Bang Bang You Are Dead

Saul Warshaw

Full Moon Publishing, LLC

Glade Spring, VA

Website: http://www.fullmoonpublishingllc.com

Cover image by Bridgeforth Designs

ISBN: 0692530185
ISBN-13: 978-0692530184

CONTENTS

THE YEAR; 2001

Chapter One

"Do you know who Carl Clemson is?" Jack Goodman asked as I came into his law office in Encino, California, first thing in the morning.

I was there because Jack had called me last night, asking if I could see him as soon as possible. When Jack wants a meeting, it's because he has investigative work he needs done. And that's where I come in.

I'm Will Jonas, a retired Los Angeles Police Department homicide detective, and now into the sixth year of running my private investigations company. Although "company" is sort of an exaggeration, there being only two of us as members.

There's me. And there's Rose Shapiro, my secretary-telephone operator-receptionist-bookkeeper-researcher-Jewish mother-person.

"Everyone knows Carl Clemson," I said. And then I sang the words to Clemson's late night TV commercial. "If your car needs parts…come to Carl Clemson. Car parts at Clemson."

"Ugh," Jack warned, "don't sing that again. I've got enough heart burn without your adding to it."

The commercial ran almost endlessly at night, on the independent, cheap-buy television channels in Southern California. One or another version of it had been on, since the early 1970's, when Clemson opened his first store. I remember reading somewhere that Clemson Automotive now had 18 stores.

"I promise. But only if what you have for me is big enough to be worth my coming down here, all the way from Woodland Hills."

"All the way? What? A whole nine miles? You getting too old to drive?"

I ignored Jack's comment and sat down in a chair on the

1

visitor side of his desk. Jack pushed a file folder toward me.

"This one's hot, Will."

"Because...?"

"Because someone's threatening to kill Clemson."

"Gee, I didn't think the commercial was that bad."

"Someone is not happy with the man," Jack said. "He's getting threatening letters. And in the last few days, some phone calls, too. Clemson called me, and asked if I knew a good private detective. Against my better judgment, I recommended you."

"Thanks, of course. But this is something Clemson should take to LAPD."

"He has. And they're working on it. But Clemson wants his own investigator, too. He's the kind of hardnosed guy who likes to use every resource he can, when he's got a problem."

Jack nodded at the file.

"So, do you want the job?"

"Does a bear shit in the woods? Sure I do." I tapped the file. "Who's handling it for the Department?"

"A Detective Soto. Manny Soto. In the Devonshire station in Northridge."

"Too bad."

"You know him?"

"Yeah. Operates by-the-book. Never met a form he didn't love to fill out. Just the kind of tight-ass I have a rough time working with."

"Clemson is paying $175 an hour, plus expenses, with $2,500 in fees up front."

"I can work with Soto."

Hey, for that kind of money, I could work with almost anyone, even though I knew Soto would be difficult. He doesn't have much use for guys like me, who leave the Job and go over to the rent-a-cop side. Never mind that I put in my thirty years. That doesn't count with the Soto types.

"Why'd Clemson call you about this?" I asked Jack. He's a good solo practitioner, but not typical of the kind of multi-named, downtown law firm that I guessed Clemson would use for his corporate work.

Jack looked at me with mock indignation.

"Lucky for you, I won't take that question as an insult. And to answer it -- I represented the owner of a couple of store sites Clemson wanted to buy. As a result of the negotiations, Clemson quite correctly was impressed with my capabilities."

"Quite correctly?"

"You're patronizing me."

"Quite correctly."

Jack laughed, and right there is one reason I like the guy. How many lawyers do you know who laugh? Especially at themselves?

"So," I continued, "can you give me some background on Clemson? Sure I know who he is, but no details."

Jack thought for a while before answering. Typical lawyer.

"Self-made, all the way. Born and raised in some small town in Central California. Very smart. Ruthless as hell, although he covers it over with a good sense of public relations.

"His life revolves around Clemson Automotive. Like they say, he lives, breathes and eats it.

"Married to the same woman forever. Has two sons – both in the business with him. And a daughter. Don't know much about her. Clemson's in his mid - 60's, but never slows down. From what I saw during our real estate negotiations, his sons are ciphers. Daddy runs them, just like he runs the company. His way is the only way."

Jack's description gives me a jolt. Not a big one, though, because I'd learned to control the emotion over the years.

Why a jolt? Because Clemson sounded like a duplicate of my father, same type of you-got-to-do-it-my-way person.

He and I fought like hell, once I reached my teens. And he was the reason I enlisted in the Corps on my 18th birthday, though it meant going to Viet Nam.

Things got a little better when I came back from Nam. But we were never close. Two hardheads butting, and no one winning. That would describe it.

"You with me, Will?" Jack's question brought me back to the present.

"Sure."

I thought about what Jack had told me.

"You know, Clemson sounds like the kind of guy who'd have plenty of business enemies. Could be – one of them might be pissed off enough, to send him those letters."

"That's for you to find out, Sherlock."

I tried to think of a clever comeback to Jack's comment, but I couldn't.

So, I left without saying goodbye. He deserved that.

Chapter Two

From Jack's Encino office to mine in one of the Warner Center business buildings in Woodland Hills isn't much of a haul, and with the light, mid-morning traffic on the 101 Freeway West, I made it in 12 minutes.

Rose greeted me in her usual manner

"Nu? Where have you been? You didn't let me know."

Does that sound like a Jewish mother? Well, that's how Rose is. Been that way from the first time she walked into my office, over five years ago.

I'd asked some placement office to send over candidates for an everything-assistant, it was the end of the day, and I was tired, after interviewing the six airheads who'd come in.

And then Rose marched in. Rose never walks. She marches. In those sensible, soft-soled, low cut, lace up shoes.

I took one look at this 60-plus, gray-hair-tied-in-back, short and round lady, and decided the last thing I needed was this grandmother who should have been off in some senior center, cruising in her rocking chair.

But Rose saw things differently. She usually does, as I was about to learn.

"You look like hell," she told me. "Sit! And don't move."

Then she made me a great cup of coffee and I hired her. Hadn't had coffee like that for almost four years, ever since my wife, Vera, had died.

I apologized to Rose.

Sorry, but I had an early morning meeting with Jack Goodman. He's recommended me for an assignment with Carl Clemson. You know, Clemson Automotive?"

"Every time I need oil," Rose said.

I'd take ten to one odds that Rose didn't even know how to open the hood on her car, let alone find the oil dip stick, but I was afraid I'd lose.

"That's the one," I confirmed.

"What is the assignment?"

"Clemson is getting threatening letters and phone calls. He wants to know who's behind it."

"So, you'll want the usual news clip file on him? Going back how far?"

"Start with six months.

"And call Clemson's office and set up an appointment. Not till tomorrow, though. I want to see Manny Soto at LAPD before I meet with Clemson. And I want to go through the file that Jack gave me."

Now that I was through with Rose, I called Soto, to arrange to see him. He said now would be a good time, so out I went, but not before telling Rose where I was going. Didn't want her to worry, you know.

Chapter Three

As I drove north on Reseda Boulevard, across the San Fernando Valley, toward the LAPD station on Devonshire in Northridge, I thought back to when I was working cases with my partner, Charlie Black.

How we operated used to drive the station brass crazy – especially Captain Klinger, our commander. He was one of those by-the-book types, and Charlie and I weren't.

We'd do whatever was necessary to solve our cases. Nothing too illegal or nasty. But we bent the rules when we had to. And we got the bad guys. And isn't that what it's all about?

Given our different sizes and builds – Charlie is round, five nine and 195 pounds, and I'm big and solid at six four and 210 – Charlie usually was the good cop and I played the bad one.

Now, thinking about my meeting with Manny Soto, and his by-the-book mentality, I told myself – adapt, Will. Go with his style. Not yours.

Nuts, I answered myself back.

Luckily, that's as far as my self-argument went, because I'd arrived at the station. I drove to the back of the building, parked near a row of black and whites, and went in,

Walking through the squad room, on my way to Soto's desk, I saw a few familiar faces and exchanged some friendly backslapping and shoulder punching. Got the juices going some, I have to admit. Yes, I'd turned my badge in voluntarily. Still, every time I came into a station, I got the itch to check the board and see what was going on.

When I reached Soto's desk, he was, what else, working on a pile of paperwork. He was friendlier than I expected, and I learned why, when I sat down and Soto started talking.

"Carl Clemson knows the Chief. He knows the Mayor. He knows the whole damn Police Commission. Otherwise, I wouldn't be wasting my time, talking to you. I don't believe in civilians investigating crimes."

I gave him my best smile. The really big, sincere, ear-to-ear grinner.

"Look, Manny," I humbled myself, "I won't get in your way.

7

I know how things work, and I promise I won't cause any problems."

What I said thawed Soto from frigid to cool. He picked up a folder and handed it to me.

"Everything you need to know is in there. Copies of the letters Clemson received. A list of possible suspects we got from questioning Clemson. But there isn't much to go on."

"Nothing useful in the letters?"

"Computer printed. Narrows it down to how many million printers? No fingerprints, except Clemson's. He didn't think to keep his hands off of the letters when he got them. Of course, since there were no other prints, the fact that he handled the letters doesn't mean shit."

"You think the letters and calls are a serious threat? Or just some crank?"

"Who knows?" Soto shrugged. "I mean, the way things are, rich businessmen like Clemson can be prime targets for extortion."

"Done a lot in Europe."

"Right," Soto agreed, "And with all these Russian Mafia shitheads coming into the country now, who knows? So I gotta take this seriously from that standpoint."

He nodded toward the file he had given me.

"And yeah, I'm paying attention to this case because of who Clemson knows. I don't need anyone bitching to the Chief about how I'm handling things."

I didn't envy Soto the politics. And I knew I better be sensitive to the situation, too. Cover my own ass.

"You find anything promising, you come right to me with it, understood?" Soto said.

It was more a command than a question.

"Sure thing," I said.

But my fingers were crossed when I said that, so my promise didn't count, right? Rules are rules, you know.

On my way out, I saw that Charlie Black wasn't at his desk, and I knew where I'd find him. And sure enough, there he was, standing by my car.

Charlie is the only person I know who can put on a freshly cleaned suit in the morning, and by noon, have it look like he'd slept in it. Rumpled, was the right word for Charlie. But smart as hell, is how I'd describe his mind.

"So, how do you like it over here?" I asked Charlie

He'd recently transferred from West Valley in Reseda to the Devonshire station in Northridge.

"It's good. A little quieter, maybe. I like it."

Then Charlie smiled.

"Have a good time, talking to Soto?"

"Like going to the dentist."

I shook my head.

"Actually, it was okay. He's got everyone looking over his shoulder, so he has to treat me right, because he knows Clemson hired me."

"Too bad we're not working this one together," Charlie said wistfully.

"Hey, whenever you want, there's a spot waiting for you."

"Yeah, I know. Just not ready yet."

Charlie changed subjects.

"Will, anything I can do to help you on this one…"

"I know."

Chapter Four

I left the Devonshire station, drove west on Devonshire to Tampa Boulevard, and then south, toward home. That was in Tarzana. In a condo that my wife, Lucy and I had. Or more correctly, the condo was Lucy's, and I had moved in three years ago, about six months before we got married.

Lucy is the first woman I've been close to, since my wife, Vera, died six years ago. We met at a night class I was taking at Cal State, Northridge, in how to operate a computer. Lucy, who is a software programmer for a bank in Encino, was the instructor, and I was the dumbest person in the class. A complete Neanderthal, when it came to computers. Which is why she had to spend so much time at my desk, explaining things. At least, that was the reason in the beginning. But then, I asked her out for coffee, and the rest, as they say, is history.

Lucy met me at the door, holding my glass of club soda. Yes, I'm a recovering alcoholic. Sober for close to six years. I don't make a big deal of it, but you should know.

I took the glass, drank, and then looked with appreciation at this wife of mine. A real looker, as they say. Lucy is five feet nine inches without heels and she weighs 136 pounds. Her hair is, of course, red. What else, with a name like McClellan? The face? Angular, with a model's high cheek bones. A perfect nose, too.

I smelled something cooking, and I guess the concern showed on my face.

Lucy saw it.

"Don't worry, it's just lasagna. Even I can't ruin pasta, right?"

Debatable point, I thought, but wisely didn't say.

When we met, Lucy told me she avoided kitchens, including her own. So we mostly ate out. Fine with me. Except in the last few months, Lucy had decided she'd like to learn how to cook.

I told her that at her age, 42, that was a pretty late start time. And with me being 57, I wasn't sure how many lousy meals I'd want to eat.

Wrong thing to say, of course, because it made Lucy all the more determined to cook. And so, tonight we were eating lasagna

– which turned out to be pretty good. Not Fab's-on-Reseda good, but better than I'd expected.

Over dinner, I told Lucy about my new case, and asked her, "Ever see or meet Carl Clemson?"

As the top computer programmer in her bank, Lucy often was included when management was pitching a company, for new business. As Lucy explained it, "Our Number One would point to me and say our computer people certainly can 'talk the talk' with your computer people."

"Then I'd rattle off a few phrases no one in the room understood. And that was the end of my part of the pitch."

"But did I ever meet Clemson? Yes, I've been at a few dinners where he was up on the dais, but that's about as close as I've gotten. I understand he's a real powerhouse, though."

"I'll find out tomorrow," I said uneasily.

Why my uneasiness? Truth is, every time I think about Clemson and his kind of control-it-all power, I get pictures of my father cluttering up my mind. I don't like the feeling.

"What's the matter, Will?" Lucy asked, picking up on my mood.

"Nothing."

"Sure. And that's why you look like that."

"Like what?"

"Apprehensive. Yes, that's the right word. You look apprehensive."

I got up from the dinner table and started walking around the room. Old habit of mine. Got to walk when I talk.

"When you're a cop, especially in Homicide, you meet all kinds of characters. And some are about as rough as they make human beings. They never bothered me. But every once in a while, there'd be a guy who, goddamn it, reminded me of my father…and…how he used to beat the physical, and the mental, shit out of me."

I shrugged.

"I can handle it. But it pisses me off, to still get that feeling."

I forced a grin.

"So, here I am, 57 years old, and I'm still letting my father beat up on me. You think I should grow up?"

"No, I like young men."

11

Lucy walked over to the couch in our living room, sat down, and patted the place next to her.

"Stop walking," she told me, "come over here, sit down, and let's neck. Do young people do that anymore?"

"They do a lot more than that," I said.

"We can, too," she assured me.

Chapter Five

The next day, before meeting with Carl Clemson, I went through the file Manny Soto had given me.

First, the letters. There were three of them. All printed on plain white, 20 pound paper. The kind used for computer printers, and pretty much untraceable.

Sure, the manufacturer probably could be found, if someone wanted to bother analyzing the fiber content and other elements. But that would be a no-brainer and a waste of time. I guessed the number of sheets of paper produced every year got up into the hundreds of millions, maybe billions. Go follow that trail, huh?

The content of the letters didn't give up anything worthwhile. No mention of a specific beef the writer had with Clemson or Clemson Automotive. No references to any past relationships. Maybe having worked for Clemson Automotive? Or having been a vendor to the company? Or a customer at one of the Clemson stores?

Nothing to point me toward any suspects.

I'd read plenty of threat letters over the years, and by comparison, the ones to Clemson were the most clueless I'd ever seen.

About the only thing that did come across in all three letters was a general threat, based on what seemed to be a hatred of rich people. This sentence, or one like it, was in every letter.

> "People like you, with all your money, deserve to be
> punished. And it has to hurt. You must experience
> pain. And you will."

I wondered if these might just be crank letters, from some nut case who had randomly picked Clemson's name out of the papers as someone rich. Someone he hated, just because of Clemson's money. I knew from the background file Rose had prepared for me that Clemson received a lot of publicity. Just a few months ago, he'd been profiled in one of those Sunday, LA. Times business section stories on successful businessmen and how they got there.

Another reason this might be a crank, and I thought this could be an important point, is because the letter writer didn't ask for anything. The writer had a lot of anger, and was directing it at Clemson, but he never said what he wanted Clemson to do.

Did I say "he?" Wrong. Couldn't rule out that the letter writer might be a woman. Not likely, in my experience, but not impossible.

The one taped telephone call also didn't give up any good clues. Soto had told me the voice was heavily disguised. Couldn't tell if it was a man or a woman, no accent, and the words were said so slowly, it wasn't possible to analyze the speech pattern.

I had to agree with Soto, when I listened to the tape.

"I hope you have gotten my letters. I hope you are worried.

You should be. There is much for you to worry about in the future.

You will hear from me again. Your time is coming."

That last sentence got my attention.

"Your time is coming."

Put that together with the reference to…"it has to hurt"…and…"you must experience pain"…and it looked to me like the writer, by the time he made that call, had some action in mind. And whatever it was, it posed a threat to Clemson.

I wondered some more about the person's motive. On that telephone call, the threatener still had not asked for anything.

Why?

Why no demands?

Does he want money?

Or is he involved in some cause or movement, and he wants Clemson Automotive to change some policy it has, because it doesn't agree with the cause or movement?

Sure, no responsible organization would operate that way. But every cause has its share of fringe nuts.

Could that be what was going on here?

And then, what about that other possibility Soto and I talked about? The Russian Mafia? Could this be a gang effort to extort money from Clemson? Business people in Russia regularly got extortion threats – and they were followed up by kidnappings and killings. Hadn't happened here, yet. But could this be the start?

All in all, a lot to think about, as I went to meet with Carl Clemson.

Chapter Six

Clemson Automotive was in a building on Jordan, between Devonshire and Lassen in Chatsworth, in an area zoned for offices, light manufacturing and warehousing. From Rose's notes, I knew the building was owned by Clemson, and that there were offices in the front, with shipping and warehousing in back.

I parked in the front, went in through the double glass door entrance, and told the receptionist I had an appointment with Carl Clemson. A couple of minutes later, I followed his secretary down a hallway and into a large heavy-on-the-dark-wood-and-leather office, where I was met by three men.

The oldest of them held out his hand.

"Mr. Jonas, I'm Carl Clemson."

Clemson was about six feet tall, built broad and beefy, but not fat. He had thinning gray hair combed straight back, his face was tanned and lined, and his nose was a bit on the long side, almost Roman. His eyes, under bushy eyebrows, were direct and hard, and I felt my insides were being x-rayed.

Clemson smiled, but there was nothing warm about it. Then, without looking at them, he pointed to the other two people.

"And these are my sons, George and Stanley."

George Clemson, in contrast to his father, was about five feet, nine inches, and wet, he might have weighed about 160 pounds. He had stringy, light brown hair that he was starting to lose, his handshake was nothing to write home about, and he avoided looking directly at me.

Stanley Clemson, the younger son, looked more like his father. He was tall, and he had his father's general build but with an extra 20 pounds, all of which looked fat and soft.

Both sons mumbled their hellos as Clemson took my elbow and guided me to a couch. The wall behind the couch was loaded with pictures of Clemson with politicos, local, state and national, as well as Hollywood types and jocks. Like Soto said, Clemson seemed to know everybody. Most people call this a "brag" wall. I call it an "ego" wall, and it was clear to me that Clemson had a big one.

Clemson sat down in a chair facing the couch, where I sat, and

George and Stanley, who were trailing behind us, went to a couple of nearby chairs.

"I appreciate your taking on my case, Mr. Jonas," Clemson began, "and I assume the purpose of this meeting is to fill you in on the details?"

Despite his strong presence, and all of his buddies on the wall behind me, Clemson seemed a bit nervous, but I figured that was understandable, given that someone was threatening him.

"Call me Will," I answered. "And yes, I do want to ask you, and your sons, some questions."

"They don't know much," Clemson said, nodding at his sons. "Not sure how productive it will be, talking to them."

I looked over at George and Stanley. Both were staring down at the floor. Neither contradicted what their father said, and I remembered how Jack Goodman had described them.

"Ciphers," he'd called them.

And they sure weren't doing anything to make me think Jack was wrong.

But Clemson's comment about his sons made me realize that I needed to let him know who was in charge. You see, in any investigation, if you let the victim call the shots -- decide what you do, who you talk to -- you're sunk before you start. No matter how sharp that victim is, his or her outlook is all screwed up – just because he, or she, is the victim. So, letting that person tell you how to conduct the investigation is a lousy idea.

"My experience," I explained to Clemson, "is that everyone connected with a case probably knows something that might help. I'm sure that includes George and Stanley, here."

Clemson stared at me for a beat or two. And I swear, I saw my father in that stare. The way he used to look at me, when he wanted something done his way, which was always.

I got zapped again by that jolt deep in my stomach, but I pushed my father into a far part of my brain and stared back at Clemson.

He broke first.

"As you wish," he said.

I turned to George and Stanley.

"Catch up with you later?"

Both looked at their father, and when he nodded, they got up and left.

I pulled out Soto's file.

"I've read the police file," I told Clemson, "and the first question I have is this. How come you waited until the telephone call, to notify the police? Why didn't you call them when you got the first letter? Or the second? Or even the third?"

Clemson shrugged.

"That first letter, I thought it probably was from a harmless crank. I grew more concerned with each new letter, of course, and I'd just about made up my mind to go to the police, when I received that telephone call. And now, I am concerned.

I asked him, "According to the police report, you can't think of anyone who might be behind this?"

"That's right," Clemson confirmed.

"Someone like you, successful in business, you've probably stepped on some toes. How about someone you crossed in business? A competitor? A supplier? Anyone like that?"

"Yes, of course I've had some rough dealings with people, with other companies. But nothing that would warrant this kind of attack, threats like these."

I tried a different angle.

"These are unusual letters," I said.

"I'm...not sure I understand," Clemson said, growing a bit nervous, edgy.

Couldn't blame him, of course. Getting a series of threatening letters could set anyone on edge. And now here we were, getting down to the nitty gritty, and talking about the letters, specifically.

"It has to do with motive," I explained. "Letters like these, threatening letters, are usually written because someone wants something. Maybe it's money. Or revenge. Or the letter writer feels he's been wronged, somehow. Or maybe it's something he wants your company to do. But there are no demands in these letters. Or in the telephone call. In other words, no motive."

Clemson thought about what I'd just said.

"Well, maybe a demand will still come? In another letter?"

"I hope so. A letter with some kind of demand, might give us a clue about who the writer is."

"Are you saying that we have to wait for another letter – if there even is another letter – before you can do anything?"

"No. The letters are only one area of investigation. There's plenty more to consider."

"Such as...?"

I figured now was as good a time as any to ask what people call, "the delicate question."

So I asked it.

"What about your private life? Is there anything there, that could make someone threaten you?"

Clemson stared at me. He knew what I meant, and it obviously was making him angry. Too bad, buddy, I thought. It's a legitimate question. I decided to state it even more plainly.

"What I mean is, have you had any affairs with women you've dumped? Who might be bitter enough to want some kind of revenge?"

Clemson continued to stare at me.

Then, "I know what you mean" he snapped. He leaned toward me. "I do not play around."

"Okay," I said. "Sorry for asking, but I had to run it down."
Hey, he's the client. Have to give him some respect, right?

I went back to the file.

"You gave the police a list of business associates, competitors, suppliers, the usual groups of people to check in a case like this. Since giving them the list, have you thought of any more names?"

I handed him a copy of the multi-paged list. He studied it, then handed it back to me.

"No. This is a complete list. Nothing to add."

Next, I asked Clemson, "Your company is very successful. Maybe there's someone who wants to do harm to it? As some sort of revenge on you?"

Clemson gripped the arms of his chair, and his voice was harsh and threatening as he answered me.

"I built this goddamn company from a two by four store. It means everything to me. Anyone messes with my company, they'll be more than sorry."

He took a deep breath, calmed down and shook his head. "But no, I can't think of anyone like that. The list I gave the police – the one I just reviewed – has all of the names I can think of."
I closed Soto's file,

"That's about all I need for now," I told him, "Although I'm sure I'll be back for more. Also, I want to interview your wife. Could you please let her know that I will be calling?"

"Is it necessary for you to talk to her?" Clemson countered. "Emily isn't a very…strong person. She's already upset about this, and I'd like to spare her any more stress."

"It is necessary. I'll make it short and sweet. But like I said before, everyone connected with the case might know something."

Clemson nodded.

"All right. I'll tell Emily to expect your call."

Clemson was quiet for a few seconds. Then he leaned forward and stared hard at me.

"I want you to understand something. I've hired you because, when something involves me, I expect to, I am used to, I need to, know everything. I'm sure the police are proceeding in an efficient manner. But I want to know what is happening, in real time, when it happens. And that's why I'm paying you. To check out everything. And to report everything back to me. Is that clear?"

"As a bell," I promised.

But my fingers were crossed, and you know what that means. The guy was paying me, but he didn't own me. Sure, I'll keep him informed. Sure, I'll do as good a job as I can for him. But I'll decide what to tell. To who. And when.

The meeting was over.

As I started to get up, I leaned forward a bit on the soft cushion of the couch seat, to give myself some leverage, and that's when I saw something on the carpet, under a corner of Clemson's desk.

I walked over to the desk, bent down and picked up a small pill bottle, the kind that pharmacies use for dispensing prescriptions. Nosy guy that I am, I sneaked a look at the label. It was from the Madison Avenue Pharmacy in New York, the prescribing doctor was R. Ghajar, and the medication was something called Avinza.

I held the bottle out to Clemson.

"This yours?"

Clemson took the bottle and looked at the label.

"Yes," he said, putting the bottle into his suit jacket pocket. "Damn allergies. These help some."

See? Even the rich have the sniffles.

Chapter Seven

George and Stanley were waiting for me in George's office, just down the hall from their father's. They were sitting quietly, George behind his desk, Stanley in a chair facing the desk. I sat down in a chair next to Stanley.

"Your audience with the Pope over?" George asked sarcastically.

"We had a good meeting."

I decided to flick at that sore spot that was so obviously irritating George. See what might come out.

"Your father's quite a man," I said, putting just enough admiration in my voice.

George looked at me. He was upset, seemed very up tight. I wondered if he was on drugs. Being a recovering alcoholic, I usually can spot someone who is using, and it looked to me like George might be a candidate.

Before George could say anything, Stanley answered.

"We know our father has accomplished a lot. He never let's us forget it."

Uh huh, I thought. Not only are these two ciphers, like Jack Goodman said, they also are very bitter ciphers. Bitter enough to send those letters to their Old Man? Maybe even thinking about doing more than just letters and telephone calls? Definitely something to think about.

"It's none of my business," I said, "but it looks like you two are pissed at your father. Any particular reason?"

George stared at me. Angrily, he swiped at a couple of strands of hair that had fallen on to his forehead.

"I hate him! And I hope whoever is writing those letters, means to do something more. Like kill him!"

"George," Stanley warned, "You don't want to talk like that!"

"Why? Because he'll hear me?" George shook his head. "I don't care. I just don't care anymore!"

I decided a little calming might be a good idea.

"I'm sure you can work things out with your father, George." George grunted, but said nothing more.

So much for my calming effort. Time to get back to the questions I wanted to ask the two of them.

"Either of you have any idea who might be sending those letters to your father?"

"The police asked us that," Stanley said, "but we couldn't think of anyone."

"Your father is a tough businessman. He's probably rubbed some people the wrong way. Anyone come to mind? Someone who had a bad run-in with your father?"

Again, Stanley answered.

"We gave the police a few names. But we told them we didn't think any of those people would do something like this. They, and our father, had some difficulties, but they're businessmen, and we don't believe they could write those letters."

I looked over at George. He was compressed into his chair, almost like a little kid trying to hide from something he didn't like, staring at nothing that I could see. I spoke to him, in a loud voice that I hoped he couldn't ignore.

"George, you're the president of the company, and Stanley is vice president, right?"

George nodded.

"Do either of you know of any employee who might be angry enough to write those letters? Or maybe someone who's been fired, and has a grudge against your father and the company?"

Neither of them answered.

I decided to shift over to family matters. Maybe I'd get something useful there.

"I'm going to see your mother," I told them. "What does she think about those letters your father's been getting? What's her opinion? She concerned?"

"My mother," George came out of his reverie to answer, "doesn't have opinions. My father tells her what to think."

"About everything?"

"About everything," Stanley confirmed.

"What about Joan, your sister? Where does she fit in? Is she in the business?"

"The only smart one among us," George said. "She got out."

"Joan's not involved with Clemson Automotive?"

"Not at all," Stanley answered. "She never even tried. And the way Joan and my father don't get along, it wouldn't have worked, anyway."

I decided it was time to leave this dynamic duo, so I got up, but George held up his hand for me to stay.

"You don't think he'll let you do your own investigation, do you?" he asked.

I played dumb.

"I don't know what you mean," I said,

"What I mean is, anything my father is involved with, he has to run it, control it."

George waved his arm around.

"Just like he controls this company. Yeah, I'm president and Stanley is vice president. But so what? It doesn't mean shit. We don't run anything. We don't make any decisions. He makes them all. He controls everything. Us included. And he'll get to you, too.

George looked at me for a few seconds, then he swiveled his chair toward the window and stared out at his own private world, wherever that was.

I looked at Stanley. He looked back at me, then down at the floor.

Nothing more for me, here, I decided, so I left. Leaving George looking out the window, and Stanley staring at the floor.

It was hard to believe that these were two grown men. Grown in years – yes – but thanks to their controlling father, they'd never grown up emotionally. It was easy to see, that the Clemsons were one helluva dysfunctional family.

Chapter Eight

"I didn't know you were familiar with terms like 'dysfunctional family,'" Lu said to me.

We were having dinner at our favorite delicatessen, Art's in Studio City. Good food and damn the two C's – calories and cholesterol.

"Are you insulting me?" I asked.

"Just teasing," she answered.

"Sometimes they're the same thing and it can hurt," I said.

"Hope it doesn't affect your appetite," Lu said, reaching over to my plate to take a forkful of my potato salad.

I waved my fork at her.

"Away from there, Woman," I warned. "Back to that green stuff on your plate."

Lu had much more eating discipline than me. I ordered all the good stuff at Art's – after all, why go there to eat lettuce? Lu had ordered a tuna salad plate. Of course, this was maybe the fifth time in ten minutes that she was pirating from my assorted deli platter, but who's counting?

"Kind of hard to believe what you're telling me," Lu said in a more serious tone. "In this day and age, a father who can so completely dominate his children?"

"I guess if you start on them early, and keep at it hard, and long enough, you get what you want."

"Two sons who do whatever Daddy says? Period?"

"Looks that way to me," I told Lu. "They're both beaten down to nothing. And George, the older one, I'm not sure how much in touch he is, with reality."

"But they're in the company, aren't they? How do they function?"

"As near as I can tell, they do whatever their father wants them to do. I guess in that way, they can function okay. Just carrying out their father's orders."

Lu made another stab at my potato salad, but I beat her off. My fork over hers. Temporary victory.

"I can't imagine a father like that," Lu said, accepting her defeat gracefully.

"I can."

"Yours?"

"Yup. But my father was minor league, compared to Carl Clemson."

"How so?" Lu asked,

But I didn't want to get into any details, and Lu could see that, so she changed her line of questioning.

"Clemson have any idea who's threatening him?"

"No, but I'll tell you this. If whoever is writing those letters does anything to hurt Clemson Automotive, I think Carl Clemson would use every dollar he has, to find and to punish that person. His dedication to Clemson Automotive is complete. He lives, breathes and sleeps that company. I'm sure he cares more for it, than for his family."

"Love your company more than your wife? Or kids? Pretty sad, isn't it?" Lu said.

She looked over at me, and suddenly, she seemed a little nervous.

"What's the matter?" I asked, actually putting a forkful of potato salad on her plate.

She ignored the potato salad. And now, I knew we were into something serious.

"I have to go out of town," she said

"So?" I prompted.

"Well, it could be for a...a long time..."

I stopped eating, which is something I rarely do at Art's.

"How long...is a long time?"

"Maybe for about two months. It's in connection with a bank we're acquiring in Ohio. I've got to check out their entire computer system. Main office is in Columbus. Branches around the state."

Ohio brought back some heavy memories for me. About three years ago, I'd busted a gang of Mafioso from Cleveland, Ohio, who were trying to set up an international child pornography network in Los Angeles. Several of them had gone to prison.

Lou reached across and took my hand

"Will, this is going to be the first time that we've been separated, since we were married. And for such a long time. I tried to get out of it, but – well..."

"You have to go," I told her. "It's important to your career, and you have to do it."

I squeezed her hand.

"Hey, it's not like we're a couple of 20 year old newlyweds. With separation issues."

Lou squeezed back.

"I'll be able to get back here on some weekends," she said.

"It will be fine," I assured her. "When are you going?"

"In two days."

She reached across to my plate and forked up a large mound of potato salad.

"You don't mind my taking this, do you?" she asked. "Art's doesn't have a branch in Columbus."

"I know that."

"Good," she replied, now eyeing the chopped liver on my plate.

The lady does know when to push, doesn't she?

Chapter Nine

Carl and Emily Clemson lived in Silver Ridge, a gated home community in the northwestern corner of Chatsworth, a suburb that was part of the city of Los Angeles.

Carved out at the base of the Santa Monica Mountains, Silver Ridge had only custom-built mansions, each on at least two acres, and all costing a minimum of three million dollars, with several pushing toward five and six million.

Getting into Silver Ridge seemed almost like needing a passport. I had to ID myself to the guard, he called the Clemson home to verify that I had an appointment, I had to wait until the guard filled out a guest card for the inside of my windshield, and then, only then, did those Pearly Gates open, to let an outsider like me drive in. Hell, I wouldn't have been surprised if I'd been told to change my tires, so I wouldn't bring in any street dirt from the outside world.

The guard had given me a map, and following it, I had no trouble finding the Clemson home. One look at it, and I figured it was a five million dollar version.

After parking in the circular driveway, I walked up a few steps to the front door and pushed the bell. I heard chimes, and a few seconds later, the door was opened by a woman who looked to be in her late fifties.

She obviously was not the maid, and even if I had thought so, she cleared up that point by introducing herself.

"Hello, I'm Emily Clemson, and you must be Mr. Jones?"

Emily Clemson was an acceptable looking woman in a forgettable way. What I mean is, everything was there, in the right places, and the pieces did fit together, but the result didn't make much of an impression.

Her hair was short, a mix of gray and weak blond. Her face was slightly on the pudgy side, matching her age-rounded body. She was dressed in a beige skirt and blouse. Just lipstick for makeup, and a wedding band and small earrings as her only jewelry.

A few minutes later, we were seated in what I guess you'd call a den, although it was about the size of a tennis court. We were sitting down near one end, just about where Steve Sampras would be serving.

Mrs. Clemson seemed calm enough and maybe not quite as fragile as I'd expected, based on her husband and sons' comments.

"I want to thank you for seeing me, Mrs. Clemson," I began. "I'm sure all of this is a strain."

She smiled a small smile.

"Yes...but Carl says it's necessary." Another small, tentative smile. "What...is it you wanted to ask me?"

"To start with, I'll ask you the same question I asked your husband and sons. Do you have any idea who might be the letter writer?"

"No, I don't. I'm sorry."

"Well, as you think back over the years, are there any people who come to mind, who might be angry enough with your husband, to want to hurt him in any way?"

"I...don't know much about my husband's business activities, but from a personal standpoint, I can't think of anyone. I'm sorry," she added.

Mrs. Clemson was in to a lot of apologizing, you can see.

I looked around the room.

"You have a beautiful home," I told her.

She smiled. "Thank you." Then she stopped smiling. "Not at all what we started out with, and sometimes I wonder which is really better."

I sensed that Mrs. Clemson was a person whom no one spent much time listening to, and I decided to encourage her. Never know what might come out.

"How did you and your husband meet?"

Mrs. Clemson seemed embarrassed.

"I'm sure you wouldn't be interested in any of that."

"But I am," I assured her. "It could be important to my investigation. Maybe something that will point me in the right direction."

"You...think so?"

"Possibly," I encouraged her.

Mrs. Clemson relaxed a bit, settled into a more comfortable mode.

"We met when I was 17. Carl was 22, already graduated from college. We both lived in the Central Valley. Do you know that part of California, Mr. Jonas?"

"Just to pass through, on the way up to Northern California," I admitted.

"When I married Carl, I gave up going to college. Back in those days, a woman's place was in the home. At least, that's what I believed."

She smiled.

"That first year was so wonderful. Carl was working in a hardware store, pretty much running it, in fact. He'd had some talks with Mr. Peterson, the owner, about buying the business. And I was very happy, busy setting up our home. Our first home."

She frowned.

"Then, Carl came home and told me we were moving to Los Angeles. To a suburb, Van Nuys. He told me he'd bought a small auto parts store. A great opportunity, he said."

Mrs. Clemson shook her head.

"I was so concerned about the move. And when we got here, I...well...I was lonely. Carl was in the store all day, and half the night. Even then, he was always...consumed with the business. Even then, he had big plans. He started with that first store in Van Nuys. Then, within a year, he and Bill had a second store. In Reseda."

"Bill?" I interrupted.

"Bill Schlesinger. Carl's partner," Mrs. Clemson said.

"I didn't know your husband had a partner."

"He doesn't now, but for the first two stores, he and Bill Schlesinger were partners."

I don't think Mrs. Clemson realized it, but when she mentioned Schlesinger, her voice took on a bittersweet tone.

"Bill was such a nice person, and I liked him very much. He made me feel...much less lonely."

She gasped and the color rose in her face.

"Oh, please, don't get the wrong idea. There was never anything between Bill and me. We were just good friends. When I visited the Reseda store, which Bill ran, it was just so nice to talk to someone. There was really no one else to talk to."

She shook her head.

"Oh! I shouldn't have mentioned Bill. Carl gets very angry if I do. They had some kind of disagreement, after the second store was opened, and Carl bought Bill out. Carl has never wanted to talk about it. It's as if...he has decided there never was a Bill Schlesinger. Please, Mr. Jonas, don't tell my husband I mentioned Bill. Please."

The fear was clear on Mrs. Clemson's face and in her voice.

"Of course I won't," I assured her, as I wondered if this Schlesinger guy might be a suspect. He and Carl had the outs about something, then Clemson bought Schlesinger's part of the partnership. Just two stores then, now 18. A much bigger pie that Schlesinger would still have a major slice of, if Clemson hadn't bought him out. Forced him out, from the sound of it.

Could that give Schlesinger a possible motive? Revenge? Could he be the letter writer? Have to check it out.

Mrs. Clemson was kneading her hands together, obviously concerned that she had told me about Schlesinger. I tried to reassure her.

"Mrs. Clemson, what you've told me about this Bill Schlesinger? There's no need to worry."

She wasn't buying my assurances.

"Can you leave now, please? Please leave now..."

Chapter Ten

It was time for some independent sniffing and snooping.

So far, I'd gotten whatever I had from Jack Goodman, Manny Soto and members of the Clemson family, Joan Clemson still to come.

What I was looking for now, was some other-source information about Carl Clemson and Clemson Automotive – anything that might help me unravel this case, point me toward a suspect.

Yeah, sure, I had that Bill Schlesinger to look up, as a possible suspect, with revenge as the motive, because Clemson had cut him out of a good thing

And I wasn't dismissing the idea that George and Stanley Clemson might be the letter writers. They certainly hated their father. But was their hatred strong enough to overcome his absolute dominance of them? Good question.

Al Silverman was an L.A. Times reporter back when I was a homicide detective with LAPD. Al had two loves, journalism and police work. Poor eyesight had kept him out of the Police Academy, so he joined the Times, and worked his way up to being the paper's police beat reporter.

Early on, Al and I had hit it off. He was the kind of guy I could sit around with and discuss one of my homicide cases. And damn, he'd have good ideas, a fresh view on something I'd gotten too close to. We'd talk as friends, not as cop and reporter, all off the record. From time to time, though, I'd help Al on a story he was working on, by giving him some "informed source" information, something the other reporters didn't have.

Al retired from the Times about the same time I left the Job. We still kept in touch, so I knew he'd become editor of Automotive America, a trade newspaper that covered the "aftermarket." That's a fancy word for the retail stores and body shops that sell replacement parts and do repair work on cars.

This was the category that Clemson Automotive fit into, so I was hoping that Al might be able to give me some information on the company and on Carl Clemson.

After some catch-up talk – how you doing, Will, how's your family, Al – I asked him if he knew Clemson Automotive and Carl

Clemson.

"Be a pretty piss-poor reporter if I didn't," Al said. "Clemson Automotive is one of the success stories of the industry. Nothing like the nationals, such as Sears, or the warehouse operations like Price-Costco, but here in Southern California, the company's done well."

"What about Carl Clemson?"

"Callous Carl?" Al answered. "That's what he's called sometimes. A hard guy. Don't get between him and the success of Clemson Automotive. It could hurt.

"Will, what's this about? Why're you asking questions about Clemson and his company?"

"Off the record, Al? Friend to friend, like we used to do?"

"Like we used to do," Al confirmed.

I filled Al in on my investigation, leaving nothing out. I knew I could trust him.

"So I'd like to know more about Clemson, the man and the company, from some outside sources," I explained, "and that's where you come in."

"What exactly are you looking for?"

"Anything and everything. Whatever you hear around, about the company, and about Carl Clemson. I know he's a hardass, so who are his enemies? Who might want to hurt the guy? Or at least scare him with those letters? Anybody being squeezed in competition with Clemson Automotive, who might want to strike back? Or is there anyone thinking about trying to take over the company?"

"They're private, Will. Clemson Automotive's not a publicly held company."

"Yeah, I know that's a wild guess, but I have to figure every angle, you understand. Wouldn't be the first time one private company made some kind of pass at another private company."

I'll see what I can find out," Al said. "And is the other part of our relationship still on?" he asked. "Do I get first crack at any story that develops?"

"Same as always," I assured him.

Next on my list was Louis The Fisherman. Now there was a character.

If I was still on the Job, Louis would be one of my snitches. In other words, an informer. Like most informers, Louis had a police record, and it had been on one of his many arrests that I had been able to turn him, to make him agree to be an informer for me. In return, we dropped the charges we were about to book him on.

Once he became an informer, Louis wasn't like the others in that category. You know how some people are destined for great things in whatever career path they take? Well, snitching is what Louis was born to do. A real American success story. So much so, that he earned the nickname, "Louis The Fisherman." Louis would cast his nets out, trawl around, and come up with all kinds of information to sell to the police.

Of necessity – because too many people would be happy if he were dead, Louis became a master at being – nowhere. You couldn't find Louis, if you didn't know how. If you didn't have one of his ever-changing telephone numbers. That was the only way to contact Louis. Call him on one of his phones, leave a message, he'd call you back, set a place for the meet.

Notice – he – set the place. And the time. And the conditions. That was how Louis managed to stay alive -- a real accomplishment, because longevity wasn't the usual destiny of an active snitch.

Louis set the time for our meeting at 10:30 PM. He told me to go to a small industrial park in Northridge. I was to take Tampa north to Londelius and turn left into the park. Londelius wove through the park, clusters of warehouses and offices on both sides of the street.

"Go slow," he told me, "no one around at that time of night, and I'll find you."

And that's what I did. Go slow. And that's what Louis did. Find me. As I was rounding one of the curves on Londelius, he stepped out into the street. I stopped. He got in. And I started driving around the park again.

Louis looked over at me and grinned. Yeah, did I forget to tell you that Louis was a likeable guy? He wasn't like most snitches, who were sorry excuses for human beings.

"Been a long time, Will."

"True enough, Louis. Just haven't had any need for your talents, lately."

"And now you do?"

"Could be."

"Usual terms?" Louis was all business, now.

"A hundred bucks a pop," I told him, "if the information is solid. Two hundred if it's sensational."

Louis laughed.

"Ever hear of inflation?" he asked.

"According to the Federal Reserve, there isn't much," I said.

Yes, it's true. I could mention something like the Federal Reserve, and Louis would know what I was talking about. I told you he was an unusual snitch.

"I got my own Federal Reserve, Will, and I got my own kind of inflation, A hundred and fifty for good information. Two fifty for great stuff.

"No problem," I said.

"So what do you need? And who do you need it on?"

"This one's a little different, Louis. Here's the deal. I'm working with a client, a company called Clemson Automotive, and the guy who heads it, Carl Clemson. He's been getting some threatening letters, and I'm trying to find out who's sending them. And that's where I need your help."

"Clemson Automotive? They got stores, right?"

"Right. Eighteen of them, mostly here, in the L.A. area."

"You thinking extortion?"

"That's one theory. Another might be revenge against Clemson, himself. He's a tough guy, and he's probably run over a lot of people in building his business. Maybe there's someone who wants to get even. Someone who might be looking for a hired gun to do some harm to Clemson. That's a stretch, I know, but it's all I have to go on, right now. And it's one of the things I want you to be looking for. Any hired gun stuff."

I took an envelope out of my jacket pocket and gave it to Louis. He opened it and looked at the ten, one hundred dollar bills.

"You want some serious looking, Will."

"Yes, I do. And I need some fast answers."

"Ever need slow answers, Will?"

Louis pointed at an alley between two buildings we were

nearing.

"Let me off there," he told me. "I'll be in touch."

Chapter Eleven

Joan Clemson was the last family member that I needed to talk to, and I nailed her down for a meeting a couple of days later.

"I don't know what I can tell you of any use," she'd said when I called to set up the appointment. "I haven't talked to my father in a year, and I only see my mother when he's not around."

"That's okay," I told her, "something useful might come out of our meeting. Can we do it tomorrow?"

She agreed to meet if I'd come to her office in Studio City, at the advertising agency where she worked, Kendal, Dalton and Winters. When I got there, I had to wait a few minutes, so I looked through the agency's brochure that was on the coffee table in the reception area. Joan Clemson was pictured inside, with the title, "Senior Vice President/Creative Director."

I knew enough about ad agencies and the titles they use to realize that Joan was a heavy, the el numero person in charge of developing the advertising campaigns for the agency's clients. I couldn't help comparing her obvious success with the zero accomplishments of her brothers.

A few minutes later, an administrative assistant – that's what they call secretaries nowadays – led me into Joan's office. Joan came out from behind her desk to greet me, and I saw a woman who resembled both her mother and father.

She had her mother's blond hair, but Joan's was long and bouncy, looking as good as one of those hair care commercials. And she had her mother's light coloring.

Her eyes, like her father's, were piercing, but with a definite hint of warmth. Her nose, again like her father's, was a bit on the long side, straight and well proportioned for her high cheekboned face.

She had on a white blouse buttoned to the neck and topped by a large black bow. Her loose fitting, gray skirt ended just above her knees. She was perched on medium heels that I estimated brought her up to about 5 feet 9 inches in height. And I guessed her weight to be in the 125 to 135 pound range.

Altogether, Joan was a looker, although I had the feeling she didn't pay much attention to that fact.

"Mr. Jonas, you are persistent," she greeted me, extending her hand for a firm handshake along with a slight smile.

Definitely the strong character of her father, I thought, but nowhere near as cold and lacking in humanity.

"Didn't mean to be a pest," I told her."

"And you've not been. But as I said when you called, Mr. Jonas, my father and I haven't talked in a year, so I don't think I can give you any useful information. But fire away."

"Please call me Will. And let's start by my asking you the same question I asked the rest of your family. Can you think of anyone who might have some sort of a grievance against your father, to the point of threatening him with those letters and that call?"

"And you please call me Joan," she said.

"Well, as I'm sure you know by now, my father is a difficult man who no doubt has made his share of enemies. But I can't think of anyone who would be that aggravated with him, to send those threatening letters. Of course, you understand that I know very little about the inner workings of Clemson Automotive. I have nothing to do with the company."

"That's too bad," I said, "because it looks to me like you're the only one of the children who could be of use there, who could work with your father."

"I must say, you are pretty direct, and I guess you mean that as a compliment. But it could never happen, I assure you. I decided a long time ago, that my life wasn't going to be one where all the decisions about me, were made by someone else."

"Specifically, your father."

"Specifically, my father,"

"Both George and Stanley said you were the smart one, for having gotten away from your father and the business."

"I don't know if I'm the smart one. I only know that I never could function under the conditions they face every day. I love my brothers very much. And I try to see them, both, as often as possible."

She sighed.

"And I guess I am lucky, because unlike them, I did manage to break away. It saddens me every day, to see how George and Stanley do hurt. And my mother, too."

"You and your father don't talk at all?"

"It's been about a year since we had our last argument, at which point I stopped trying to have any sort of relationship with him. I'd kept trying up to then. For the sake of Mother and my brothers. But it wasn't to be."

"And no interest at all in being part of Clemson Automotive?"

Joan smiled.

"Well, if I ever need anything for my car, I do make it a point of buying it at a Clemson Automotive store. And I even pay retail."

"Wouldn't want to hurt the profits, right? By getting a discount?"

She laughed.

"Oh, I'd never want to hurt the profits of Clemson Automotive. My trust fund and those of my brothers are dependent on those profits."

"Trust funds? First I've heard about trust funds. Can you please tell me more about them?"

"Sure. All of us, George, Stanley and I, have trust funds. Our father set them up about 15 years ago, when he started to get very rich."

She sighed.

"Of course, in his usual, controlling way, he set up those trusts so that we can't get to them for quite a while. The age when we can take them over is, would you believe, 55."

"You mean, you can't get at the trusts, or take anything out of them, until you're at least 55 years old?"

"That's right. I did some research, and most trust funds in this country are given over to the recipients by about age 30 or 35. But not with my father. He controls our trusts until we're each 55."

"Why?"

"Do the math, Will. I'm 32 now, so I have 23 years to go. Stanley is 34, so it's 21 years for him. And George is 37, and that's 18 years for him. Now, my father is 63, so when George is able to take over his trust, in 18 years, my father would be 81. For Stanley, he'd be 84. And by the time I can access my trust, in 23 years, he'd be 86.

Joan leaned forward for emphasis.

"Get the picture, Will? It could well be, that Dear Old Dad will be Dear Dead Dad before any of us come into our trust funds."

I shook my head and said, "Pretty grim. He's trying to keep

control over all of you, even from the grave."

Joan laughed.

"Hey, Will – look what I just gave you. Motives for George, Stanley and me to want to hurt our Father – to write those threatening letters and make that phone call."

I stared at Joan and she stared right back at me. I saw the math, but I didn't see any capability among the three children, to do any sort of real damage to their father. Of course, I'd have to give some more serious thought to the whole deal, but my first impression was – that this was not their gig – either individually or as a group.

"Uh uh," I protested. "The three of you being aggravated? Sure. But doing this sort of thing? I doubt it."

Joan asked, "And you've made your decision so fast because...? I'm really curious."

"Because it would be stupid for the three of you to start down that path, with those letters and the phone call. Or to go forward with anything more after that. Why? Because the trust fund angle would immediately put the spotlight on you, as suspects. Like you yourself called to my attention, the three of you all have motive."

I leaned toward Joan and smiled. After a few seconds, she smiled back. I wagged my finger at her.

"Joan, you're having a good time teasing me."

She laughed.

"Guilty, I admit it." She turned serious. "The trick is, Will, not to let it get too grim when discussing our trust funds. If I do, then he's winning. He's controlling. So, any time I can put some humor into a trust fund discussion, I'm tempted. My apologies, for having done so with you. Please excuse my behavior."

"No need to apologize. You've got a great attitude about it."

Joan looked at me with those piercing eyes.

"You married, Will? Or going with anyone?"

"Married. And happily so."

"Too bad. All the good ones are always taken."

"Hey, I'm old enough to be your father."

"Would that you were," she shot back, laughing. "We'd probably have a better relationship than the one I have with my present father."

Joan leaned forward in her chair.

"Tell me, Will, do you think these letters and the call are serious? Or just some crank?"

"I keep bouncing back and forth on that," I admitted. "Anyone as prominent as your father, well, the letters have to be taken seriously."

"So, why do you have your doubts?"

"Because these letters are unusual in one important respect. There've been three of them, now, and the phone call. All threatening. But nowhere is there any demand for anything. Not for money. Not for any change of corporate policy. That's unusual. And very puzzling."

"What do the police say?"

"They're at the same place I am. We're working our leads, our hunches, but nothing concrete yet."

"As I said before," Joan mused, "my father has made many enemies in business. I'm sure you're looking in that direction?"

"The police are more into that, than I am," I told her. "It's easier for them, as cops, to get to see corporate executives. I've got a meeting with LAPD tomorrow, and if there's anything worthwhile to report I'll let you know."

"Thank you."

Joan glanced at her watch. I caught the movement and got up.

"I don't have anything more I want to ask you now. Probably want to talk with you, again, though."

"Anytime," she assured me.

I left, thinking about the trust fund angle. And where did I come out? Well, it sure did provide a motive – for all three children – but I still couldn't see it as being viable. Have to give some more thought to it, though.

As for Joan Clemson? I liked her. The first family member I'd met who seemed solid, and nice and decent.

How she'd managed to be that way, in that family environment? Go figure. I sure couldn't.

Chapter Twelve

Late the next afternoon, I went to the Devonshire Station to meet with Manny Soto. I told him about the family trusts, and he said he already knew about them, and he had pretty much decided the three children, pissed as they were, were not up to the role of real bad guys. In other words, there was motive but there wasn't a deep and dirty enough capability to carry out any meaningful operation against their father. I wasn't as sure about this as Manny was. I still wanted to do some more thinking about it.

Otherwise, the meeting wasn't too productive.

Soto did tell me that "We've checked every which way, and we're pretty sure there's no Russian Mafia involved. Strong-arming corporate executives may be their style in Russia, but not here. We're eliminating that angle."

And I could just see Manny, bookkeeper that he was, crossing out the Russian Mafia line on his list. I could see it, but of course, I didn't say anything.

"What about you?" Manny asked. "What've you turned up?"

"Nothing much. I've met with all the Clemson family members. I know you did, too. And I got zilch."

Well, that wasn't entirely true. I did learn about Bill Schlesinger, but I wasn't about to give that up to Manny. I wanted to check Schlesinger out myself.

"Been almost a week now, since that last telephone call," Manny said.

"Yeah, and I'm thinking what you're thinking," I told him. "There should have been another letter, or call, by now."

"Right."

We were both silent for a few seconds, until Soto spoke again.

"Not for publication, but the Captain told me to ease up on the manpower on this one. It's looking more and more to us like a crank deal."

Sotto's announcement was good news to me. I hadn't been happy from the start, going over the same ground as the Department. Now, it looked like I'd have more of a clear field to operate in.

Soto asked, "You're still doing your thing for Clemson, right?"

"So far."

"And our understanding's still the same," he warned. "You learn anything useful, you come to me with it. Right?"

"Right," I answered.

But it was finger-crossing time behind my back, Folks.

After finishing with Manny, I schmoozed in the squad room with Charlie Black and some other guys I knew, so by the time I went out to the parking lot, it was after six. I thought about going home. Only Lu wasn't there. She was in Ohio, working on that bank merger deal. Been only two days since she left, and I was really missing her. Love, huh?

So I decided to go back across the Valley to my office in Warner Center. Get caught up on my other clients. I'd been shortchanging them all week, because of the Clemson Automotive case.

But then, I didn't have to go back to the office, because the office came to me. A call on my pager. I checked the number. It was the special one Rose punched in, when she wanted me to contact her, pronto, so I got in my car and called on my car phone.

"I've got five messages here from Carl Clemson in the last two hours. He says he has to see you," Rose told me. "And how come you haven't been answering your pages?"

"Because I turned my pager off while I was in with Soto. He doesn't like little beep-beeps upstaging him during a meeting."

"I think you should go to Clemson's office right away," Rose advised. "He sounded irritated. He said to tell you that he'd wait for you, no matter what time it was."

"On my way," I told Rose.

It was less than a ten-minute drive from the Devonshire Station in Northridge to Clemson Automotive in Chatsworth. When I arrived, the parking lot was empty, except for cars in the three assigned spaces belonging to Carl, George and Stanley.

I parked, got out of my car and walked up to the glass double door entrance. It was empty inside. No receptionist. But the door wasn't locked, so I went in.

It was quiet. With no one to announce me, I started walking

down the corridor toward Carl's office, which was at the end of the corridor. About three quarters of the way down, I heard loud voices coming from Carl's office. Carl and his sons were yelling at each other. I stopped and listened. I'm a detective, right? A snooper. So I snooped.

George was shouting.

"But why didn't you tell us about it?"

Stanley added, "It was embarrassing to find out from the other company!"

"It's none of your damn business!" Carl snapped.

"None of our business?" George shouted again. "You decide to sell Clemson Automotive, you start talks with Acme, and it's none of our business?" George's tone was close to hysterical.

"What the hell are you worried about?" Carl snarled. "Your pension? About Barbara being able to keep spending like she does? Don't worry. That'll all be taken care of."

"It isn't any of that," Stanley implored. "We're supposed to be the management of this company, and...you never tell us anything."

"I tell you what you need to know. And what you've earned the right to know."

"You've never given us a chance to learn. To succeed," George shouted. "You have to control everything! Everything!"

Listening to the argument, I thought...George, you got that right. Here was a prime example of their father walking all over them. Something he apparently did all the time.

"You two listen," Carl ordered. "I've heard enough of this shit. I'll tell you what I want to tell you, and that's that. Now get out of here! I've got more productive things to do, than waste my time talking to you."

Figuring George and Stanley would exit Carl's office any second, I looked around for somewhere to duck into. There was a door to my right. I tried the handle. It wasn't locked. I opened the door and went into someone's office. I left the door open just a bit, and saw George and Stanley come out of Carl's office.

Pissed off. Angry. Beaten down. All of those terms applied to the Brothers Clemson. And I wondered if maybe Manny Soto – and yes, me – were being a bit hasty in discounting the possibilities of George and Stanley being the letter writers. Like they say, "If

/ill, it's 2001 now, right? By about 2010, it'll be all big
l outfits dominating the market."

nought back to the argument between Carl Clemson and his
hey had been complaining about Carl holding talks to be
d by Acme. At the time, it struck me as odd that Carl
be willing to be acquired by anyone. He'd be giving up
, and that would be hard for a control freak like him.

w, with what Al was telling me, it made more sense. If
on Automotive was having financial problems, then selling
another company could be a solution. Carl Clemson would
lenty of millions from the sale, and that could soothe any
ion he might have, about no longer being in charge, no
being in control of things.

o," Al asked, "do you have anything for me yet? Something
uild a story around?"

espite my promise to Al, and I was going to keep it, now was
time to tell him about the discussions Carl was having with

ve learned a few things, Al," I told him. "And they're
o be useful to you. But I can't say anything yet. Okay?"

kay," Al agreed. He knew I wouldn't screw him. And he
ht.

ter I hung up, an out-of-left-field thought hit me. I
red if there was any connection between what Al had told
ut Clemson Automotive having cash flow problems, Carl
on having acquisition discussions with Acme, and the
ning letters.

hat kind of connection? What would make sense? Who the
ew? Probably no connection. But I decided I needed to
is one some more thought.

w, though, it was time for me to demonstrate what an ace
ve I was. How I could take the knowledge gained from my
ears on the Job, and my three years as a private detective,
ply it to solving something.

be specific, I wanted to find Bill Schlesinger. In my book,
on's former partner was as good a suspect as I had. So l was
o talk to him, never mind that Carl said not to.

w to find the guy?

new that Schlesinger and Clemson were partners up through

looks could kill…"

I waited until the two brothers went down the hall and into George's office, and then I went to Carl's office and looked in.

He was seated at his desk, reading a file. And unlike his sons, so upset by the shouting match, Carl was calm, composed, in control.

I suspect that's the way Ivan The Terrible looked, after he gave the order to cut off the head of some Russian nobleman. Hey, I bet you didn't know I watched the History Channel.

I knocked on the side of the doorframe and Carl looked up. When he saw me, a look of annoyance crossed his face.

"Come in," he ordered.

I walked in and sat down on the opposite side of the desk from him.

"I've been trying to reach you for hours," he said.

"I was at police headquarters, meeting with Detective Soto," I explained. "At meetings like that, I turn off my pager. I'm sure you understand."

He didn't want to understand, but since I'd tied my explanation to a meeting at LAPD, he didn't have much choice. Couldn't complain about my doing work on his behalf. Score one for me.

"What did you learn?" he asked.

"Not much. Detective Soto told me they'd checked out the local Russian Mafia types. They extort businessmen like you in Russia. But he doesn't think they have any connection to this situation."

"And I know you've been busy, checking with the members of my family," Clemson interrupted.

"As I told each of them, and you, it's the best starting point for me. Trying to find out if any of you can think of people who might be behind this. The police have been checking on the business side of things, with people at other companies. Soto tells me they've got some leads to run down, but so far nothing solid."

Clemson nodded.

"There's one thing I want you to – not – pursue," he directed.

"Oh?"

"When you met with Emily, she told you about Bill Schlesinger."

"Your former partner."

"Only in a minor way. Just on the first two stores. And they were bottom level operations. Anyway, if you were thinking of contacting Schlesinger, don't."

Just like my father, I thought. Give the order, no reason necessary. I reacted to Clemson's order the same way I used to react to my father's orders.

"Why?" I asked.

Clemson looked at me. The piercing eyes shtick.

"Because you work for me and I've told you so."

Still the stare. Then he waved his hand dismissively.

"But I'll give you another reason. Schlesinger and I haven't had anything to do with each other in thirty years. There's nothing he can tell you that would be of any interest. Or use. So, don't see him. Understood?"

"Understood," I said.

But guess where those fingers of mine were?

Chapter Thirteen

The next day, I was in my office, working on a file for one of my clients, when Rose stuck her head in.

"Al Silverman is on line two. Do you want to take it? Or to call him back, after you finish with that file?"

"Take it," I told her, putting the file down on top of a pile of other files.

Rose looked disapprovingly at the pile.

"You have been picking up those files and putting them down for two weeks now. Enough with the schlepping. Finish those files, so I can put them away. Is that too much to ask?"

"I love you, Rose. Will you be my mother?"

"If I thought that could happen, I would leave this earth for a spiritual rebirth. Maybe in Palm Springs."

"I can't think of a nicer place," I told her.

"Believe me, you would miss me."

She left, and I wondered if maybe, someday, I'd win one of these discussions with Rose. I can hope, can't I?

"Hello, Al," I said, picking up the phone. "Watcha got?"

"What I got, are little things here and little things there, and they add up to something that could be interesting."

"Like?"

"I think Clemson Automotive may be in a bit of a fi[nancial] bind."

"How do you figure that?"

"Well, one of the best ways to learn about a company, its suppliers, the people who sell the goods, the product i[n] to that company."

"And…"

"In the automotive aftermarket, the suppliers are getting paid in thirty days. That's the way the system wo[rks] of them operate on tight margins, don't have a lot of cas[h] need, and expect, to get paid within 30 days of delivery."

"And some of Clemson Automotive's suppliers aren['t]"

"And some aren't. They're mostly smaller sup[pliers] can't yell as loud as the big vendors, and they're bei[ng] wait, for up to forty five days."

"And that's because Clemson Automotive is havi[ng] problems? Not because Carl Clemson has decided to [ ] whole payment process and squeeze the little ones? [ ] style."

"Not even Carl Clemson is tough enough t[o] system," Al said. "No, the deal always is, the suppl[iers] in thirty days. If they don't, first they yell. Then th[ey] their deliveries. And if they really get worried abo[ut it] they only deliver c.o.d. – cash on delivery."

"Is that happening to Clemson Automotive?"

"No c.o.d.'s yet, but a couple of the supplie[rs] about it, unless Clemson gets them back on a thir[ty] schedule, and soon. Of course, Will, I'm not too su[re] I learned," Al added.

"What do you mean?"

"Companies like Clemson Automotive are ha[ving a] harder time staying in business. Clemson is pretty [ ] know they have eighteen stores in their chain. B[ut] compete with the powerhouses that have come [ ] years. The warehouse operations, like Price [ ] national chains, like Sears."

"So," I asked, "bigger is how it's all going [ ] like Clemson get swallowed up by a larger co[ ] under?"

Clemson Automotive's second store. That store was in Reseda, and the first one was in Van Nuys. Both locations were in the San Fernando Valley.

So it seemed to me that the chances were good that Bill Schlesinger, at least at that time, was living in the Valley. And if he was then, he still might be. Of course, he might have left the Valley, or retired into a senior citizens home somewhere, or maybe even died. But let's think positive.

I walked over to one of the bookshelves in my office, where Rose kept phone books from all parts of the Los Angeles area, and searched for the San Fernando Valley books.

The first one I picked up covered the northern part of the Valley. I went to the "S" pages and looked for "Schlesinger." There were seven of them, but no "William" or anything near it.

Now on to the directory covering the southern part of the Valley, which I saw included Van Nuys and Reseda. Better luck here, There were twelve "Schlesingers," including two with the first name of "William," one with the first name of "Willard," and one with the initial, "B."

Back to my desk and the telephone.

I hit it on the third call.

"Hello," a man answered when I dialed the "Willard" Schlesinger number.

"Hello," I said. "I'm looking for a Bill Schlesinger who used to be with Clemson Automotive. Could that be you?"

There was a pause at the other end.

Then the man asked, "Who is this?"

"My name is Will Jonas. I'm a private investigator, and I'm looking for a Bill Schlesinger who used to be partners in two of the Clemson Automotive stores, in Van Nuys and Reseda. Is that you?"

Again a pause, then, "Well, you found me. Now, what's this all about?"

"Mr. Schlesinger, I'm glad I've located you. Can we talk? Can I come and see you?"

"Why?"

Of course, I wasn't going to tell the man that the reason I wanted to see him, was to find out if he was writing threatening letters to his old partner. No, I didn't think that would get me an appointment.

"I'd like to discuss things in person," I said. "I got your name from Emily Clemson, and it's tied in with her."

I remembered how fondly Emily had spoken about Schlesinger, and I was betting the feeling might have been mutual. I was right.

"Okay," Schlesinger said.

He gave me his address in Van Nuys and we set an appointment for two o'clock tomorrow afternoon.

Chapter Thirteen

I was in the office around 5:30 that night, going over those files Rose had been yelling at me about, when the phone rang. Rose was already gone, and I almost let the call ring through to the night answering service, but I picked it up, and I was glad I did. It was Lu, calling from Columbus, Ohio,

"I see you're staying out of trouble, working hard, while I'm away," she said in greeting.

"Hey. How are you? I was going to call you a little later."

"I'm fine. But it's already 8:30 here, so I decided to call before going out for some dinner."

"I keep forgetting Ohio is three hours ahead of California. How's it going?"

"Hectic. Meetings. Meetings. And more meetings."

Lu paused, then continued. "I miss you, Will," she said softly.

"I miss you, Lu."

Another pause.

"Gee, just like a couple of kids," Lou joked.

I asked, "Can you come back for the weekend? Or should I come there?"

"Unfortunately, not a good idea," Lu said. "We're going at it, seven days a week. And, I don't know where I'll be later this week. Either Cincinnati or Cleveland."

Lu's voice took on a mock sexual growl.

"Too bad, though. I've got a big double bed here, for us to play on."

"Well, if you're still stuck out there, maybe the weekend after?"

"Plan on it. Please."

She shifted subjects.

"So, what's new on the Clemson case?"

One of the nice things Lu and I have found, is that we can talk to each other about our work. It's the short of shop talk that sometimes helps each of us sort things out, look at new ideas, new angles.

So, I gave Lu the latest details, and then asked her that question I'd asked myself, after I talked to Al Silverman.

"Here's what I'm wondering. It probably makes sense to

think that there's a connection between Clemson Automotive's cash flow problems and the fact that Carl Clemson is talking to Acme about being acquired. Do you agree?"

"Sounds reasonable."

"But what about this? Is there any connection between those two things, and the threatening letters Clemson's been getting?"

"Why would you think that?"

"No specific reason. Only, here's Clemson in business for what, over thirty years? Pretty big time for the last twenty years, and no one threatens him or his company. Now, when he's got cash flow problems and he's talking acquisition by a bigger company, that'll get him out of trouble, now's when the letters come. So, could they possibly be from someone who is a supplier to Clemson, who somehow found out about the acquisition discussions? One of the smaller ones who Clemson has been slow to pay? This person's company might be hurting bad, because of those slow payments. Might even have gone bankrupt, and all he wants to do now, is hurt Clemson Automotive.

"Or, maybe the letter writer is someone inside Clemson Automotive, who found out about the Acme acquisition talks, and wants to screw them up, for a reason we don't know. Maybe that employee is angry about having been passed over for a promotion? Or, worried about his or her job if Acme acquires Clemson? Or someone who's got a grudge against Carl Clemson, personally. With his management style, I'm sure Clemson's beaten up on plenty of his employees.

"And it seems to me, that if Acme were to find out about the letters, they could have second thoughts about the acquisition. Who wants to buy a company owned by someone who's getting threatening letters?"

Lu asked, "What about your idea that the sons could be the letter writers?"

"I've thought about that some more, and I don't think they have the balls for it."

"Then, who?"

"Damned if I know."

"Well, here's an equally crazy thought," Lu offered. "You've told me how much of an ego Carl Clemson has. And I think it's safe to assume that the continued success of Clemson Automotive looks could kill…"

I waited until the two brothers went down the hall and into George's office, and then I went to Carl's office and looked in.

He was seated at his desk, reading a file. And unlike his sons, so upset by the shouting match, Carl was calm, composed, in control.

I suspect that's the way Ivan The Terrible looked, after he gave the order to cut off the head of some Russian nobleman. Hey, I bet you didn't know I watched the History Channel.

I knocked on the side of the doorframe and Carl looked up. When he saw me, a look of annoyance crossed his face.

"Come in," he ordered.

I walked in and sat down on the opposite side of the desk from him.

"I've been trying to reach you for hours," he said.

"I was at police headquarters, meeting with Detective Soto," I explained. "At meetings like that, I turn off my pager. I'm sure you understand."

He didn't want to understand, but since I'd tied my explanation to a meeting at LAPD, he didn't have much choice. Couldn't complain about my doing work on his behalf. Score one for me.

"What did you learn?" he asked.

"Not much. Detective Soto told me they'd checked out the local Russian Mafia types. They extort businessmen like you in Russia. But he doesn't think they have any connection to this situation."

"And I know you've been busy, checking with the members of my family," Clemson interrupted.

"As I told each of them, and you, it's the best starting point for me. Trying to find out if any of you can think of people who might be behind this. The police have been checking on the business side of things, with people at other companies. Soto tells me they've got some leads to run down, but so far nothing solid."

Clemson nodded.

"There's one thing I want you to – not – pursue," he directed.

"Oh?"

"When you met with Emily, she told you about Bill Schlesinger."

"Your former partner."

"Only in a minor way. Just on the first two stores. And they were bottom level operations. Anyway, if you were thinking of contacting Schlesinger, don't."

Just like my father, I thought. Give the order, no reason necessary. I reacted to Clemson's order the same way I used to react to my father's orders.

"Why?" I asked.

Clemson looked at me. The piercing eyes shtick.

"Because you work for me and I've told you so."

Still the stare. Then he waved his hand dismissively.

"But I'll give you another reason. Schlesinger and I haven't had anything to do with each other in thirty years. There's nothing he can tell you that would be of any interest. Or use. So, don't see him. Understood?"

"Understood," I said.

But guess where those fingers of mine were?

Chapter Thirteen

The next day, I was in my office, working on a file for one of my clients, when Rose stuck her head in.

"Al Silverman is on line two. Do you want to take it? Or to call him back, after you finish with that file?"

"Take it," I told her, putting the file down on top of a pile of other files.

Rose looked disapprovingly at the pile.

"You have been picking up those files and putting them down for two weeks now. Enough with the schlepping. Finish those files, so I can put them away. Is that too much to ask?"

"I love you, Rose. Will you be my mother?"

"If I thought that could happen, I would leave this earth for a spiritual rebirth. Maybe in Palm Springs."

"I can't think of a nicer place," I told her.

"Believe me, you would miss me."

She left, and I wondered if maybe, someday, I'd win one of these discussions with Rose. I can hope, can't I?

"Hello, Al," I said, picking up the phone. "Watcha got?"

"What I got, are little things here and little things there, and they add up to something that could be interesting."

"Like?"

"I think Clemson Automotive may be in a bit of a financial bind."

"How do you figure that?"

"Well, one of the best ways to learn about a company, is to ask its suppliers, the people who sell the goods, the product inventory to that company."

"And..."

"In the automotive aftermarket, the suppliers are used to getting paid in thirty days. That's the way the system works. Most of them operate on tight margins, don't have a lot of cash, so they need, and expect, to get paid within 30 days of delivery."

"And some of Clemson Automotive's suppliers aren't?"

"And some aren't. They're mostly smaller suppliers who can't yell as loud as the big vendors, and they're being made to wait, for up to forty five days."

"And that's because Clemson Automotive is having cash flow problems? Not because Carl Clemson has decided to slow up the whole payment process and squeeze the little ones? It'd be his style."

"Not even Carl Clemson is tough enough to change the system," Al said. "No, the deal always is, the suppliers get theirs in thirty days. If they don't, first they yell. Then they slow down their deliveries. And if they really get worried about being paid, they only deliver c.o.d. – cash on delivery."

"Is that happening to Clemson Automotive?"

"No c.o.d.'s yet, but a couple of the suppliers are thinking about it, unless Clemson gets them back on a thirty day payment schedule, and soon. Of course, Will, I'm not too surprised by what I learned," Al added.

"What do you mean?"

"Companies like Clemson Automotive are having a harder and harder time staying in business. Clemson is pretty fair sized. You know they have eighteen stores in their chain. But they just can't compete with the powerhouses that have come along in recent years. The warehouse operations, like Price Costco, and the national chains, like Sears."

"So," I asked, "bigger is how it's all going? And companies like Clemson get swallowed up by a larger company, or they go under?"

"Will, it's 2001 now, right? By about 2010, it'll be all big national outfits dominating the market."

I thought back to the argument between Carl Clemson and his sons. They had been complaining about Carl holding talks to be acquired by Acme. At the time, it struck me as odd that Carl would be willing to be acquired by anyone. He'd be giving up control, and that would be hard for a control freak like him.

Now, with what Al was telling me, it made more sense. If Clemson Automotive was having financial problems, then selling out to another company could be a solution. Carl Clemson would make plenty of millions from the sale, and that could soothe any frustration he might have, about no longer being in charge, no longer being in control of things.

"So," Al asked, "do you have anything for me yet? Something I can build a story around?"

Despite my promise to Al, and I was going to keep it, now was not the time to tell him about the discussions Carl was having with Acme.

"I've learned a few things, Al," I told him. "And they're going to be useful to you. But I can't say anything yet. Okay?"

"Okay," Al agreed. He knew I wouldn't screw him. And he was right.

After I hung up, an out-of-left-field thought hit me. I wondered if there was any connection between what Al had told me about Clemson Automotive having cash flow problems, Carl Clemson having acquisition discussions with Acme, and the threatening letters.

What kind of connection? What would make sense? Who the hell knew? Probably no connection. But I decided I needed to give this one some more thought.

Now, though, it was time for me to demonstrate what an ace detective I was. How I could take the knowledge gained from my thirty years on the Job, and my three years as a private detective, and apply it to solving something.

To be specific, I wanted to find Bill Schlesinger. In my book, Clemson's former partner was as good a suspect as I had. So l was going to talk to him, never mind that Carl said not to.

How to find the guy?

I knew that Schlesinger and Clemson were partners up through

Clemson Automotive's second store. That store was in Reseda, and the first one was in Van Nuys. Both locations were in the San Fernando Valley.

So it seemed to me that the chances were good that Bill Schlesinger, at least at that time, was living in the Valley. And if he was then, he still might be. Of course, he might have left the Valley, or retired into a senior citizens home somewhere, or maybe even died. But let's think positive.

I walked over to one of the bookshelves in my office, where Rose kept phone books from all parts of the Los Angeles area, and searched for the San Fernando Valley books.

The first one I picked up covered the northern part of the Valley. I went to the "S" pages and looked for "Schlesinger." There were seven of them, but no "William" or anything near it.

Now on to the directory covering the southern part of the Valley, which I saw included Van Nuys and Reseda. Better luck here, There were twelve "Schlesingers," including two with the first name of "William," one with the first name of "Willard," and one with the initial, "B."

Back to my desk and the telephone.

I hit it on the third call.

"Hello," a man answered when I dialed the "Willard" Schlesinger number.

"Hello," I said. "I'm looking for a Bill Schlesinger who used to be with Clemson Automotive. Could that be you?"

There was a pause at the other end.

Then the man asked, "Who is this?"

"My name is Will Jonas. I'm a private investigator, and I'm looking for a Bill Schlesinger who used to be partners in two of the Clemson Automotive stores, in Van Nuys and Reseda. Is that you?"

Again a pause, then, "Well, you found me. Now, what's this all about?"

"Mr. Schlesinger, I'm glad I've located you. Can we talk? Can I come and see you?"

"Why?"

Of course, I wasn't going to tell the man that the reason I wanted to see him, was to find out if he was writing threatening letters to his old partner. No, I didn't think that would get me an appointment.

"I'd like to discuss things in person," I said. "I got your name from Emily Clemson, and it's tied in with her."

I remembered how fondly Emily had spoken about Schlesinger, and I was betting the feeling might have been mutual. I was right.

"Okay," Schlesinger said.

He gave me his address in Van Nuys and we set an appointment for two o'clock tomorrow afternoon.

Chapter Thirteen

I was in the office around 5:30 that night, going over those files Rose had been yelling at me about, when the phone rang. Rose was already gone, and I almost let the call ring through to the night answering service, but I picked it up, and I was glad I did. It was Lu, calling from Columbus, Ohio,

"I see you're staying out of trouble, working hard, while I'm away," she said in greeting.

"Hey. How are you? I was going to call you a little later."

"I'm fine. But it's already 8:30 here, so I decided to call before going out for some dinner."

"I keep forgetting Ohio is three hours ahead of California. How's it going?"

"Hectic. Meetings. Meetings. And more meetings."

Lu paused, then continued. "I miss you, Will," she said softly.

"I miss you, Lu."

Another pause.

"Gee, just like a couple of kids," Lou joked.

I asked, "Can you come back for the weekend? Or should I come there?"

"Unfortunately, not a good idea," Lu said. "We're going at it, seven days a week. And, I don't know where I'll be later this week. Either Cincinnati or Cleveland."

Lu's voice took on a mock sexual growl.

"Too bad, though. I've got a big double bed here, for us to play on."

"Well, if you're still stuck out there, maybe the weekend after?"

"Plan on it. Please."

She shifted subjects.

"So, what's new on the Clemson case?"

One of the nice things Lu and I have found, is that we can talk to each other about our work. It's the short of shop talk that sometimes helps each of us sort things out, look at new ideas, new angles.

So, I gave Lu the latest details, and then asked her that question I'd asked myself, after I talked to Al Silverman.

"Here's what I'm wondering. It probably makes sense to

think that there's a connection between Clemson Automotive's cash flow problems and the fact that Carl Clemson is talking to Acme about being acquired. Do you agree?"

"Sounds reasonable."

"But what about this? Is there any connection between those two things, and the threatening letters Clemson's been getting?"

"Why would you think that?"

"No specific reason. Only, here's Clemson in business for what, over thirty years? Pretty big time for the last twenty years, and no one threatens him or his company. Now, when he's got cash flow problems and he's talking acquisition by a bigger company, that'll get him out of trouble, now's when the letters come. So, could they possibly be from someone who is a supplier to Clemson, who somehow found out about the acquisition discussions? One of the smaller ones who Clemson has been slow to pay? This person's company might be hurting bad, because of those slow payments. Might even have gone bankrupt, and all he wants to do now, is hurt Clemson Automotive.

"Or, maybe the letter writer is someone inside Clemson Automotive, who found out about the Acme acquisition talks, and wants to screw them up, for a reason we don't know. Maybe that employee is angry about having been passed over for a promotion? Or, worried about his or her job if Acme acquires Clemson? Or someone who's got a grudge against Carl Clemson, personally. With his management style, I'm sure Clemson's beaten up on plenty of his employees.

"And it seems to me, that if Acme were to find out about the letters, they could have second thoughts about the acquisition. Who wants to buy a company owned by someone who's getting threatening letters?"

Lu asked, "What about your idea that the sons could be the letter writers?"

"I've thought about that some more, and I don't think they have the balls for it."

"Then, who?"

"Damned if I know."

"Well, here's an equally crazy thought," Lu offered. "You've told me how much of an ego Carl Clemson has. And I think it's safe to assume that the continued success of Clemson Automotive is important to feeding that ego. Now, if anyone finds out that Clemson Automotive is having problems, that's going to reflect negatively on Carl himself. And maybe that's what's behind this letter writer? An effort to scare Carl by threatening to reveal his company's problems publicly? That would damage Carl's reputation as a hot-shot businessman, and it would definitely bruise his ego."

"But the letter writer hasn't made that threat," I pointed out. "Hasn't even mentioned any financial problems Clemson Automotive might be having."

"Not yet. But maybe in a future letter? Maybe the writer is waiting for when he, or she, feels is exactly the right time. What do you think?"

"Well, it's no wilder a theory than I've come up with," I answered.

"It's the best I can do on an empty stomach," Lu said. "Will, I'm going to hang up and go to dinner."

"I sure wish I was having it with you," I told her.

"So do I." Lu paused, and then added softly, "Good night, Will."

I sat back in my chair, savoring Lu's call. But my sweet memories were almost immediately interrupted as the phone rang again.

Let it go to the answering service, I told myself.

But after thirty years on the Job, where I'd always picked up a ringing phone, day or night, it was hard to break that habit. So I answered the phone.

"Will?"

I recognized Manny Soto's voice.

"Yeah, Manny."

"Clemson's dead. Murdered."

"Carl Clemson is dead?"

"No. Not Carl. George Clemson."

Chapter Fourteen

When I got to Clemson Automotive, the building was lit up. Several black and whites, roof lights flashing, were standing at all angles in the parking lot, along with a couple of unmarked police cars.

A yellow, scene-of-the-crime tape surrounded the building. The tape reached out of the parking lot, to the street, where its ends were tied to two rubber stanchions, forming an entryway. A uniform was at the entryway.

Since Clemson Automotive is in an industrial park, there wasn't the usual crowd of curious civilians surrounding the area. But there were three television station trucks on the street.

I stopped at the entryway and lowered my window.

"Detective Sergeant Soto told me to come here. My name's Will Jonas," I told the uniform. He looked familiar.

"Right," he said. "How you doin', Will?"

I remembered him.

"Doing good, John. How about you?"

"Can't complain. Another 18 months and I have my thirty. Then it's out to Idaho."

"Lots of retired cops there. Enjoy it."

"No doubt about that," John said, moving aside one of the stanchions so I could drive in.

As I parked, I saw Carl and George's cars in their assigned spaces, but not Stanley's.

I got out, went up to the double glass doors, and repeated my story to another uniform who checked a list he was holding, and then let me in to the reception area. I walked down the hall, toward the offices, nodding along the way to those crime scene division people I knew.

Soto came out of George Clemson's office to meet me. Charlie Black was with him.

"Charlie," I greeted my old partner.

"Will," he answered.

I could see Soto was annoyed that I'd passed over him, to say hello, first, to Charlie. That meant, I figured, that Soto was in charge. His first words to me confirmed this.

"Just so you know the line of command," he said, "I'm in

charge of this investigation. Charlie is working the homicide, under me."

Behind Soto, Charlie made a shit face for my benefit. Charlie didn't like Soto any more than I did.

"Sure, Manny," I assured Soto. "I understand."

"This comes straight from downtown," Soto said. "Since I was handling the original investigation, the decision is, that I should still be in charge overall."

Soto nodded toward George Clemson's office.

"I called you over to find out if you've learned anything since our last meeting, that could help us with what happened in there."

"Mind if I take a look first?" I asked.

Soto stepped to one side,

"Just be careful."

Thanks, Manny, I thought to myself. I've only worked about a hundred of these homicides. But I promise to be extra careful because of your order. Yeah. Sure.

Inside, the crime scene personnel were covering the room. Dusting powder was everywhere, as technicians lifted fingerprints. A photographer was shooting from several angles, and all of this was being done because of a very dead George Clemson, slumped in his chair, behind the desk.

A good part of the top of his head was blown off and had spattered against the window George had been looking out of, the last time I saw him. I had wondered, then, what private world George had been looking at. Now, I didn't have to wonder. His looking days were over.

A pool of blood on the floor surrounded George's chair. There were footmarks in the blood, some leading up to the desk, and more going away from the desk and toward the door.

Charlie saw me looking at the prints.

"Those are Carl Clemson's footprints."

I looked questioningly at Charlie.

"Carl told us he discovered the body. He heard something. Didn't realize they were shots. He came in, saw George, and went over to the desk to try and help. That's when he stepped in the blood."

"Understandable," Soto added. "He panicked, of course, seeing his son that way,"

"Where's Carl now?" I asked.

"In his office," Charlie said. "A couple of my guys are with him. He's already given us a statement, so we'll be taking him home, soon. He said he wants to be the one to break the news to his wife and the rest of the family."

"You better hurry up on that," I said. "The news vultures are already outside. I spotted three TV station trucks."

"It figures," Charlie sighed.

"I'll delay giving them a statement until Carl is home with his family," Soto said.

And, I thought, but did not say, until you have time to put on a fresh shirt and tie for the cameras.

Instead, I asked, "What did Carl say happened?"

Charlie was about to answer, but Soto cut in.

"He said he was working late in his office. As far as he knew, he was the only one in the building. He thought he heard some noise. Repeated three times."

"Thought?" I interrupted. "Gun shots are pretty loud, and George's office is not that far from his."

"Let me finish," Soto snapped. "He was on the phone at the time, he told us. Starting to dial his home. He's partially deaf in his left ear, and his right ear – that's his good ear – was up against the phone receiver. And that's why he thought he heard noises, but he wasn't sure."

"And then...?" I asked.

"Well, after a while, he got curious. So, he went into the hall, and he saw that George's office lights were on. He went down there, and that's when he saw what had happened. At first, he tried to help George. But then he called 911. And the rest you know."

"No sign of any weapon?" I asked. "Any idea of caliber? Make?"

"We found three casings," Charlie said. "Might be from a 9 millimeter, a cheap Saturday night special. We're searching the building and the grounds for the weapon, but nothing's turned up yet."

"Looks like a robbery," Soto said. "George's wallet and watch are gone, and Carl says his son usually carried a few hundred in cash, and several credit cards."

"A robbery? Out here in the middle of nowhere?" I asked.

"Why would somebody come to a deserted industrial area like this, for that purpose? Better mugging opportunities in the parking lot of a shopping mall."

"There was a departmental bulletin about a similar case, about six months ago, over at the Blanton Company building on Prairie," Soto said. "The perp held up two executives who were working late." Soto smiled. He just loved to zing me. "Could be a pattern here," he said. "We also found an unlocked door in the rear of the building, next to one of the loading docks. That could be how the perp got in and got out."

"Yeah, but most muggers don't kill their victims," I argued. "With three shots. It doesn't look kosher to me."

Soto ignored what I said. He waived toward George's body.

"So, you got anything new to tell me? Anything new you've learned in your investigating?"

"I think you may be looking at this whole thing wrong," I argued again.

Soto stiffened.

"What the hell do you mean?"

"I mean, what about the possibility that this was done by the person who's been writing those threatening letters to Clemson?"

"Those were to Carl, not George," Soto said. "And besides, like I told you the last time, we're thinking those probably were sent by some harmless nut case,"

"The whole tone of those letters was a threat to Carl Clemson, telling him that he was going to suffer," I said. "To use the exact words of the writer, he said things like, 'you must experience pain,' and 'it has to hurt.' Seems to me that killing Clemson's son meets those criteria."

"We'll look at everything," Soto grumbled.

He wasn't about to admit it, but he knew I was right. Satisfaction enough for me.

"You got anything else to tell us?" he asked.

I decided I didn't.

"No."

"Okay, you can leave," he said, and he turned away and walked toward one of the fingerprint techs.

"I'll walk you out," Charlie said, grabbing my arm and pushing me toward the door of the office. From past experience as my partner, he knew I was pissed at the way Soto was treating me, and he wanted to make sure I didn't sound off. Wise move on Charlie's part,

Neither of us said anything until we were out in the parking lot.

Then Charlie growled, "I got to put up with that asshole."

"Hey," I told him, "It's a simple robbery and killing. Soto told us that. You'll have this one solved by tomorrow."

"Sure I will," Charlie sneered. Then he turned serious. "What do you think, Will? A possibility it really is a robbery and killing? Maybe no connection to those letters Clemson's been getting?"

I shrugged.

"Always possible, Charlie. Everything's there for a robbery and killing, but it doesn't add up right for me. And I can't get away from the threatening letters angle."

"Well, I'm going after all sides of it, despite what Solo thinks," Charlie said

I didn't doubt him. Charlie Black was one very good homicide detective.

He leaned toward me.

"It's between you and me, now, Will. You got anything more I need to know?"

I don't play games with Charlie.

"I'm seeing someone tomorrow," I told him. "It's a long shot, if he's involved in any of this. But I'm checking it out, and if I think there's anything for you, I'll let you know. And that goes for anything else I turn up."

"Good enough," Charlie said.

He nodded toward the building.

"I better go back in before Soto has a heart attack, wondering what we're talking about out here."

Chapter Fifteen

The next day, I was set to meet Bill Schlesinger at two in the afternoon, so I spent the morning in my office, working on one of my other clients, checking out the background of a senior level marketing executive, the client was considering hiring.

Necessary to do this kind of thing? You'd be surprised at what job applicants put in their resumes. Some of them were better fiction writers than Danielle Steele. What? You're surprised I read good literature?

After phone calls to a number of sources, I found this guy to be a real ringer. He claimed six years of consumer products marketing experience, as well as a master's degree in statistics. That's a great combination for a top-level marketing executive, the slot my client was looking to fill.

What this applicant claimed, though, and what he had, were two different things. What he had was two years as an assistant product manager in the marketing department of a small, southeastern chain of drug stores, and a bachelor's degree in marketing. Scratch this one.

I also called Joan Clemson at her office. Didn't expect her to be in, not the morning after her brother was killed. But I wanted to leave my phone number and my message, which was that I was available, if she wanted an extra shoulder to lean on.

Bill Schlesinger lived in Van Nuys, just a few minutes ride from one of the two stores in which he and Carl had been partners. His house was on one of the nicer residential streets in what's known as West Van Nuys, where people had what real estate agents call, "pride of ownership."

The homes on Schlesinger's block all came from the same cookie cutter pattern. About 1,400 square feet, three bedrooms, 1.75 bathrooms, and a back yard that could handle either a small lawn or a pool, but not both. Still, the street was attractive, because the homes, built in the late 1950's or early 1960's, had by now been customized by their owners, many of whom were the original occupants.

I found Schlesinger's house, parked, walked up to the front door and pushed the doorbell. I heard some chimes and then the door was opened by a man who said, "Hello. I'm Bill Schlesinger.

Come on in."

Schlesinger was on the short side. Maybe five eight, five nine, and slender. His hair, a mixture of light brown and gray, was thinning, but still covered most of his head. He had an open, friendly face, all the features in the right places, and no distinguishing marks. He was wearing a long sleeve mesh polo shirt, a beat up, but clean pair of chinos, and white sneakers. Not jazzy Adidas or Nikes, just plain Keds.

All in all, this guy looked like he was at peace with the world and not someone who'd write threatening letters or shoot people. Of course, as someone once said, "You never know." Who did say that, anyway?

We ended up in Schlesinger's living room, and after he'd offered me coffee, tea, or soda, and I'd said no, he asked the first question. It isn't that he beat me to it. Often, when I'm about to interview someone, I kind of wait until they ask that first question. It eases things, gives them a feeling that they are in charge. And I like that. Makes it more effective later, when I get down to the short hairs with them.

"What is going on with Carl?" Schlesinger asked. "First, you call out of nowhere, wanting to see me. And then I read in the paper this morning that George was killed last night. Is this all connected, somehow?"

"Might be."

Schlesinger looked at me, puzzled, and then in seeming disbelief.

"You don't think I killed George, do you?"

"Where were you last night? About 6:30?"

Schlesinger was angry.

"I ought to tell you to get the hell out of here! Accusing me of something like that!"

But then what seemed to be his perpetual good nature broke through his anger, and he gave a short grunt.

"But by the looks of you, you wouldn't listen. And you're too damn big for me to throw out. So, I'll give you my, what do you people call it? My airtight alibi. I was playing poker at Paul Garber's house. Started at six, broke up at eleven. Just like we do, every week, for at least the last ten years. I'll give you Paul's phone number and address to check it out. Paul will get a kick out of you thinking I killed someone. He's always saying that I don't have hard enough balls to win at poker."

I'd check out the alibi, of course, but I suspected I'd be scratching Schlesinger as a murder suspect.

But what about the threatening letters? Could Schlesinger be the writer?

Well, I still needed to do some probing, although it seemed doubtful to me that this amiable, easygoing guy could do anything like that. He was just the opposite of Carl Clemson. Made me wonder how they could have been partners. I put that question to Schlesinger.

He laughed.

"So, you can't figure how two such different types hooked up in a partnership? Well, for one thing, I don't think Carl was as much of a hardnose then, as I understand he is now. Oh, he was plenty hard driving in those days. But he hadn't lost all of his feelings for other people, at that point. Still had a little something left."

Schlesinger shifted gears on me.

"Tell me, how is Emily? I can't imagine why she brought up my name, after all these years. Is she all right? How is she coping with George's being killed like that?"

It was apparent from Schlesinger's tone that he had good feelings for Emily Clemson. I wondered how good?

"I haven't seen her since the killing," I told him, "but she was all right, when I did see her, a few days ago. I don't think she's an especially happy person, though. It looks to me like she doesn't make a move without Carl's okay, and who can be happy living like that?"

Schlesinger said, "I'm sorry for her. Always have been, But what does any of this have to do with me? I haven't seen Carl, or Emily, in over 30 years."

"Someone's been writing threatening letters to Carl, and I'm investigating it, trying to find out who."

Schlesinger laughed.

"First murder? Now threatening letters? Wow. Am I a dangerous guy. And all in one afternoon."

"I have to follow every lead," I explained. "When I was talking to Emily, she mentioned you. Said you and Carl had a falling out, and he forced you out of the partnership. You can see, that's something I'd have to look into. After all, you were forced out of a company that went on to become very big. Would have been lucrative for you. A man can get pretty angry over something like that. And it could build over the years..,"

Schlesinger nodded.

"I see your point. Yes, I was angry at the time. But I gave it up a long time ago. It would have been nice to make the money, and from that standpoint, I'm sorry the partnership ended. But it didn't end over any kind of business disagreement."

"What then?"

Schlesinger took a long time before answering.

"I'm not sure I want to tell you," he said. "It involves something that Emily doesn't know about, and I don't want to hurt her. I've always had fond feelings for Emily."

"If you tell me not to tell her, I won't. But I'd like to know what you're talking about. It might help me in my investigation."

Again, a long silence from Schlesinger, before he answered.

"Okay, here it is. I was a minority partner, had only thirty per cent of the company, so Carl didn't have any trouble buying me out. But the reason I left had nothing to do with the business. It was...Maria Gomez."

"Who was Maria Gomez?"

"She was an employee in our Van Nuys store. Parents were immigrant Mexicans. She was born here. Bright. Outgoing personality. Hired her as a cashier, but she quickly became our bookkeeper. And...well...unfortunately...she and Carl got...close."

"You're telling me Carl and this Maria Gomez had an affair?"

"That's what I'm telling you. Only from Maria's perspective, it wasn't an affair. She was in love with the guy. She was bright, but also young, just a year out of high school. And pretty innocent. Carl totally dominated the relationship."

"You're sure about all this?" I asked.

"As sure as I am about Maria's pregnancy. You couldn't miss it."

I remembered Carl's irritation with me, when I asked him about his private life, and his answer, which was," I do not play around." Well, Carl, it looks like you lied to Daddy.

"Emily didn't know about the affair?"

"Emily knew very little about anything. God, she was a young and sweet and trusting soul…fresh from the farm."

"Why did Maria Gomez' pregnancy force you out of the partnership?"

"Because I kept arguing with Carl about his duty, his responsibility to Maria. And eventually this led to a point where we could no longer work together, and he bought me out."

"What do you mean by,.. Carl's duty and responsibility to Maria?"

"Carl wanted Maria to get an abortion. Not so easy in those days, but not a problem, if you had $500, and Carl certainly did."

"And Maria?"

"Are you kidding? A good Catholic girl, except for her lapse with Carl? Catholic, immigrant parents? There was no way she could go through with an abortion."

"So, what happened?"

"Carl fired her. Gave her some money in a lump sum, and that was it, as far as he was concerned. That's when we had our biggest fight. I kept pushing him to send her more money, but that lasted only a few months. Then he forced me to sell out to him, and I was in no position, anymore, to help Maria"

"And after that?"

"I tried to stay in touch with Maria. She had a hard time of it. Her family was angry, embarrassed. But they closed around her. Took care of her, during the pregnancy, and after the baby was born, a boy. Maria named him Carlos. As in, Carl. That tell you anything? She was still, as we used to say in those days, carrying the torch for him. But it didn't do her any good."

"Carl never had anything to do with Maria and the baby?"

"No."

"You're sure?"

"Yes, I'm sure. I kept in contact with Maria, up until she died, Five years ago. Cancer. I'd know if she was hearing from Carl. And besides, if you know Carl, you know that once he makes his mind up, he doesn't change it. He decided he was through with Maria when she refused the abortion. And that was the end of it, I'm sure."

"What about the son, Carlos? He ever have anything to do

with Carl? Or Carl with him? I mean, this Carlos is the man's son."

"Again, nothing," Schlesinger assured me. "You know, in one way, they're a lot alike, Carl and Carlos."

"What do you mean?"

"They're both hard headed. Can't tell either of them anything. But Carl's turned all that hard headedness into becoming a business success. While Carlos, well, his hard head has only gotten him into trouble."

"You're in contact with him?"

"No, Maria used to tell me what was happening with Carlos. First it was juvenile delinquency stuff. Then, he got into some pretty violent arguments with people. He was arrested twice for…what do you call it ... assault and battery?"

"Battery and assault. Does Carlos know he's Carl's son?"

"Yes. Maria told me that she told Carlos, even when he was a little kid, that Carl was his father. The way she explained it to Carlos was, that Carl loved him very much, but it was God's will, that Carl couldn't come to see him."

Schlesinger shook his head from side to side.

"Pretty sad stuff, huh? I think she'd have been better off making up some phony story about a dead husband or other. But she insisted she wanted him to know the truth. I think she somehow hoped Carl would still come back some day. Or at least, acknowledge his son, and take care of him."

So, I thought, the kid lives on dreams for a while, because of what his mother told him. Then reality sets in, as he becomes a hard-to-handle juvey, and now as an adult, he's the violent type.

Would you agree, I might indeed have a new suspect for whoever was writing those letters to Carl Clemson? Hell, this Carlos might even be a candidate for the killing of George Clemson. He was violent, he was poor, he could see from any newspaper story how rich his father was. And he wanted some of that, or at least, revenge for what Carl did to his mother, and wasn't doing for him. What better revenge than to send those threatening letters, and then to off Carl's oldest son? The son who took his place when Carl cut off his pregnant mother.

I asked Schlesinger, " Do you know where I can find Carlos Gomez?"

"I haven't talked to him since Maria died. But before then, he'd show up once in a while at her house. Usually broke, He'd stay around, until he got a few dollars together. Maria owned the house. Just a plain little house in Canoga Park. Carlos inherited it. Maybe he's still there. I'll give you the address."

"Thanks."

I changed subjects.

"What about George Clemson? Did you know him? Let's see, you and Carl split up in 1962, so George was two years old."

"Cute little kid. But aren't they all? But as you say, he was only two years old, so I didn't really know him."

Schlesinger shook his head.

"Boy, did Emily have a hard time with that pregnancy, with Carl all over her, all the time."

"What do you mean?"

Schlesinger waived a dismissive hand.

"Not worth talking about, believe me. Just Carl being Carl. Wanting to control everything, as usual."

Chapter Sixteen

After leaving Bill Schlesinger, I went to check out Carlos Gomez.

The address Schlesinger had given me was in one of the crummier parts of Canoga Park. Most of the homes were beat up, and the one that Gomez owned fit right into that category. When I reached it, I parked, locked my car, and walked up to the gate of the short wire fence that surrounded the property. Inside the gate, was a dirt front yard, which at one time might have had some grass, but the only thing green now on that hardpacked surface was a large plastic garbage bag snared on one of the branches of a small bush.

I stood still for a few seconds, waiting for that large mongrel dog that I was sure was going to come tear-assing around from the back. A dog like that almost always comes with a house like this. But I was in luck. Nothing on four legs with thousands of teeth came in my direction.

I opened the gate, walked through the yard toward the house, climbed the two steps to the front door, and knocked.

Nothing.

I knocked again. Harder!

Still nothing.

I tried the door, figuring that if it was open, I'd poke my head inside and yell for Gomez.

The door was locked.

I stepped off the porch, wondering if I should walk around to the back, to see what I could see. And that's when I noticed the old man watching me. He was sitting on the porch of the house to my right.

You know the type. Thin as a rail, formless pants held up by suspenders, beat up work shoes laced half way up, a washed out, long sleeve flannel shirt buttoned to the neck, about two days' worth of grey and white beard stubble, and less teeth than you had fingers.

None of that surprised me, but what did, was when the man spoke. I'd figured this was a nice, harmless old guy, dragged up from Mexico by his kids, never learned any English, and so was stuck around the house. Instead, he spoke good English, slightly accented.

"You looking for Carlos? Not been around for a while."

"You sure?"

"Sure I'm sure. All I got to do is sit out here all day, so I know who comes and who goes. And Carlos? Not been here since the weekend."

"Do you know where he is? I need to talk to him."

"You a cop?"

"A private investigator."

"What are you investigating?"

I wasn't about to get into that. Anything I said would become neighborhood property, I was sure.

"Nothing I can go into," I told him, "but thanks for your help."

He waived and turned his attention to someone coming out of another house. Your neighborhood guardian at work!

I took out one of my cards and wrote a note to Carlos

"Carlos, I need to talk to you. It's important"

I went back up the front steps and wedged the card into the doorframe near the lock, where Carlos couldn't miss it, when he unlocked the door.

Back at my office about a half hour later I looked through the messages Rose handed me. Nothing that couldn't wait. It was more important that I talk to Charlie Black.

"How are they swinging, Will?" Charlie asked when I got him on the phone. Charlie was always the refined one.

"Can't complain," was my snappy rejoinder. I'm big on snappy rejoinders. "What's happening on the Clemson homicide? Got a coroner's prelim?"

"Right here. Like we figured, the man was shot three times with a 9 millimeter. Real overkill. Hey, you like that pun, Will? The coroner says the first bullet would have been enough."

"So why three?" I wondered.

"Don't know. Maybe the perp was nervous, not really sure of himself. So he just kept firing."

"Find the weapon yet?"

"No."

"Any charges to George's credit cards?"

"Nope."

"Now *that's* unusual, Charlie. And it's got me thinking. Like I said to Soto, this doesn't look like the usual robbery M.O., and I'm not sure that robbery was the purpose at all"

"You're back to that mystery letter writer."

"I can't get away from it," I told Charlie, "and I might even have a lead for you."

I filled Charlie in on my day, first telling him that Bill Schlesinger, in my opinion, was no longer a suspect. Then I told him about Carlos Gomez, Carl's son with Maria Gomez, and that Carlos looked like a prime suspect to me.

"I'll see what his jacket looks like," Charlie told me, "and I'll pay him a visit. See what he can tell me, about his whereabouts when George Clemson was killed."

"I left Gomez a note on his front door. If he calls me, I'll let you know. Got anything else?"

"Nothing more, except that your client, Clemson, is a real pain in the ass," Charlie complained.

"How so?"

"He's been hollering for the coroner to finish up with George. Says he wants to get the funeral over with, put it all behind him, so he and his family can go on with their lives."

"Gee, Charlie, you said that with so much sentiment. Such heart. Such feeling."

"I swear, that's what he said. Those are his words, not mine."

"But you said them so well," I teased him.

"I'm hanging up now," Charlie said.

And he did.

Rose buzzed me.

"Joan Clemson has been holding for you."

"Put her through," I told Rose, and a few seconds later Joan was on the line.

"Will?"

"Joan, I'm so sorry about George."

"Thank you, Will. And thank you for your call and your message."

"How…are you holding up?"

"I'm managing. It's all so…sudden. And I keep wishing I'd

66

spent more time with George. I'm much closer to Stanley. I…I never got that close with George."

"How's your family doing? I haven't spoken to your father, and I need to. But I thought I'd leave him alone for a couple of days."

"My father is his usual. Completely self-controlled."

I heard the tension in Joan's voice as she continued.

"He and I are barely talking, even though I've been at the house a lot ever since…this happened. Mother is in shock. Her doctor has her on tranquilizers. But it's Stanley who is most affected. I've never seen him so…nervous, almost physically shaking. He and George were very close, and it is hitting him hard."

"He'll come out of it."

"I imagine so. We all usually do, when something like this happens. Will, you said you need to see my father? You might want to come to the house, day after tomorrow. Any time after three in the afternoon, or all evening. The funeral is in the morning. A simple service. It's private. Just family. Then cremation. Condolence calls will be received by the family in the afternoon and evening."

"I'll be there," I promised. "And if you need anything in the meantime…"

"Thanks, Will. I really appreciate it," Joan assured me.

Chapter Seventeen

"So, here I am, in Cleveland, and I'm lying on the bed. I don't have anything on. The sheets are silk. Black silk. There's a mirror on the ceiling over the bed. And oh, did I forget to mention, it's a water bed? Sooo undulating."

I laughed, and at the other end of the phone line, so did Lu. She'd delivered that speech in a low, sexy, growly voice, without any preliminaries, when I'd picked up the phone.

"When your banking career is over," I told her, "you can always make a living on one of those telephone sex lines."

"You really think so?"

"I sure as hell hope not."

"I miss you, Will," Lu said, no longer joking. "I'll still be here this weekend. Can you come out?"

"Do you really have a waterbed there? With a mirror on the ceiling, and black silk sheets?"

"Afraid not. It's just a nice room in a nice motel in a section of the city called Shaker Heights."

"I'll come out, anyway."

"Well, I'm glad that's settled."

"How's the work coming along? Going to be stuck in Ohio much longer?"

"For about two more weeks. Oh darn!"

"What's the matter?"

"Nothing, really. It's just that I'm running late. Have a meeting with my counterpart. So I've got to cut this short, Will."

"Go. Go. I sure don't want to get between you and your counterpart."

"Never happen, Will. You're the one I love."

"And right back at you, Lu. I'm really looking forward to seeing you this weekend."

Chapter Eighteen

If I wasn't happily married to Lu, then Joan Clemson was a woman I could connect with. She was good looking, smart, strong and, got to admit it, sexy as hell.

Not that she was a come-on kind of lady. No big eyes promises, or open-mouth, tongue-moving, lip-wetting moves. Nope. Nothing like that. Just the opposite. She was totally straightforward, and that was one of the reasons she was so appealing to me.

But I don't want to disappoint you. There are not going to be any steamy sex scenes between Joan Clemson and me for you to pant over. Lu had that role sewed up with me.

That isn't to say that I wasn't glad when Joan called and asked if we could get together.

We were having breakfast at Mel's Diner on Ventura Boulevard in Sherman Oaks. Nothing fancy, but the food's good and basic, and when the 1950's jukebox isn't blaring, it's a place you can talk without having to shout.

"This is all your fault," Joan said, as we sat down.

"How so?" I asked.

"The voice mail you left me. Offering a shoulder to lean on."

Joan gave me a look that had "help me" written all over it

"I meant it," I assured her. "Tell me what I can do."

"Get me a new family," she joked wryly. Then she shook her head. "No, I don't mean that. What I mean is, get me a new father."

I thought back to my own father, and to the similarities between him and Carl Clemson, and I said, "Can't help you there. Hell, I wanted the same thing myself, but couldn't do anything about it."

"Your father was like mine?"

"Not on the surface. But, yes, in a lot of ways, he was. And they weren't the good ways."

We were both silent, thinking about our flawed fathers.

"He' just so damned cold," Joan finally said. "So controlling of everything around him. Even now, at this…time."

She'd been picking at her napkin with her fingernail. Now, she stopped and looked across the table at me.

"I'm spending as much time as I can at the house right now. Mother wants me there, and so does Stanley. They're like...drifting in their own worlds. Mom's mostly out of it. On the tranquilizers the doctor is giving her. I can understand that. Her love for George was something fierce."

"Her favorite?"

"Yes, but that's okay. She had plenty of love for me, and for Stanley. It's just that George was her favorite. They seemed to have some kind of a special bond between them. Maybe it had to do with George being the first-born. Or Mom's way of trying to protect George from my father's cruelties. I don't know. But once I got over the usual childhood jealousies, it didn't make any difference. I had...have...a good relationship with my mother...at least to the extent that I can, with my father around."

Joan stopped talking, but I sensed I should keep quiet. Whatever it was she had to tell me, she wasn't done yet.

"But it's Stanley I'm really worried about," she continued. "He's acting very strange."

"What do you mean?"

"Well, of course he's grieving. That's to be expected. He and George were very close. But what Stanley's going through, looks to me... like more than grieving. He seems...frightened. He's...falling apart."

A thought came to me. Not one I wanted to share with Joan. Not now, anyway. The thought? Was Stanley worried that the person who killed his brother, might have him targeted next?

Of course, that made no sense, if you go along with Manny Soto's belief that George was the victim of a robber who got an itchy gun finger.

But if you buy into my theory, that George's killing was somehow tied to the letter writer...then this did make sense. And it might be that Stanley had also come to that conclusion. And so – his frightened state. Certainly something I'd have to check out further.

My thoughts were interrupted by Joan speaking.

"Will, I wish you'd talk to Stanley. Maybe you can find out what's troubling him so much?"

"I'll try," I promised. "Maybe when I come to the house, after the funeral."

"That would be good."

I asked, "All the arrangements made for the funeral?"

"With my father in control?" Joan grimaced. "Of course. Everything is set." She shook her head. "Even down to the stupidity of the cremation."

"The stupidity of the cremation?" I echoed.

"What I mean is, dear Father decided to have George cremated. Something to do with…how horrible he looked because of…because of how he was shot…in the head, and all that. I tried to argue with him. All of us – Mother, Stanley and me – we wanted a traditional funeral and burial. But like always, Father got his way." She shrugged. "I guess it doesn't make any difference, though. Dead is dead."

Joan fought to regain her composure, and she succeeded. There was a toughness at her core, and I was glad to see it winning, over the misery and pain of George's killing, and her Father's behavior.

"I'm okay now, Will," Joan said. "I'll survive all this, I assure you."

"I never doubted it," I told her.

There was something else I wanted to tell Joan. I'd been thinking about it, ever since she'd called and asked to meet. I wanted to tell her about Carlos Gomez.

Why?

For two reasons.

First, simply because Carlos was her half brother. If I had a half brother, I'd want to know about it, because however thin that string, I was still tied to that person. That person was family to me. Call me a sentimental slob, but that's the way I see it.

And second, if it turned out that Carlos Gomez was writing the letters Carl Clemson was getting -- or worse, if he was George's killer, then I'd rather Joan already know about him, than learn in the inevitable publicity, that she had a half brother who'd done these things. Neither way was good, but I figured my way was better. So I went ahead and told her.

"I've discovered something during my investigation. Something you should know."

"What's that?"

I took a deep breath.

"You've got another brother. A half brother, actually."
Jan looked at me, clearly shocked.

I kept going.

"Your father had an affair with a woman who worked for him. A long time ago. Before any of you were born. Not too long after your parents moved to Los Angeles. The woman got pregnant, and gave birth to a boy."

Questions tumbled out of Joan.

"Where is he? Does my father know? Does my mother know? What's his name? Is he married? Does he have a family?"

I gave her the few details I'd learned from Bill Schlesinger. Joan took it all in, and she had the reaction I thought she'd have. She wanted to know more.

"I want to meet him," she told me, demanded of me. "I have to meet him."

Now came the shit part of what I had to tell her.

"You have to know something about this person. And it isn't pretty. It's possible...nothing proved yet...only a theory of mine, and I could be wrong...that this Carlos is the person who's been writing those threatening letters to your father, and...that he killed your brother."

"How do you know that," she demanded defensively. "How can you say something like that?"

"I don't know it. I'm just making some guesses. He's been in trouble with the law since he was a kid. He's poor. He knows your father is his father. And that he's rich. It all adds up to a theory. Just a theory. But one that I think can fly."

The intense pain that Joan felt after I told her this was clearly etched on her face. I watched as she tried to absorb what I'd said. Tried to make some sense out of it. I kept quiet, reached across the table and took hold of her hand. We remained that way until Joan finally spoke.

"Can things be any worse than they are now?" she asked.

This wasn't a question directed at me, but at the world. Or at least the lousy world Joan was operating in at the moment. But again, just as earlier, that inner toughness of hers won out.

"I guess it's better for me to learn this way, from you, than if something comes out during a police investigation." A deep sigh. "I need to tell Mother and Stanley."

She shook her head.

"As far as my father is concerned, he can learn on his own! How could he do that? Just walk away like that?"

I didn't have any answer to her question, and I didn't even try, as Joan continued.

"The police haven't arrested…this Carlos…yet?"

"No. As I told you, I went to his house, but he wasn't there. I've given the information to the police and they'll be picking him up, as soon as they can find him."

"You'll let me know when that happens?"

"Yes."

I was still holding Joan's hand. She eased it away and smiled at me.

"Thanks."

"For what? All the wonderful things I've told you?"

"For how you've told me."

Joan leaned forward for emphasis.

"Will, I still want to meet him. I have to meet him."

I nodded.

"Understood."

"And you'll come to the house, tomorrow, after the funeral? Please? I…need you there."

"Yes," I assured her.

Of course, I wanted to be there for her. But I also wanted to talk to Carl. And as I'd promised Joan, to Stanley.

Chapter Nineteen

Silver River was easier to get into this time. When I arrived at the gate, mine was one of a number of cars going to the Clemson's for the post-funeral reception. The guard waived all the cars through.

At the Clemson home, my car was taken by one of those eighteen year old, blond, I-live-on-a-surfboard kids. Where do the valet services find these look-alikes? Talent scouts on the beach at Malibu?

Just inside the front door, I waited in line to sign the guest book, and then followed the traffic flow into a living room about twice the size of a tennis court.

I've been at a number of wakes, or whatever you want to call them, but as many as I go to, I'm always hit by the oddity of a bunch of people standing around, eating, drinking and talking, like they're at some kind of a cocktail party.

Not much sadness. Mostly a lot of chatter, maybe a little less noisy than usual, nothing like a sense of mourning or grieving in the air. Could be that's a good thing. All part of the healing process. Get past the funeral and begin to live life again.

There had to be well over a hundred people in the room and surrounding hallways. Plenty of recognizable faces, too. In my first look around, I saw two Los Angeles City Council members, the mayor, a U.S. congressman, several industry CEO types, a couple of sports team owners, a real estate developer, and this being Los Angeles, even a few "A list" actors.

I also spotted Joan Clemson. She saw me at the same time and came across the room.

"I'm glad you're here," she said when she reached me.

"Impressive crowd. All friends of George?"

Joan scanned the crowd.

"I doubt if he knew many of the people here. But Father knows them all."

"And that's why they're here."

"And that's why they're here."

Joan took hold of my arm, and started walking me across the room.

"Mother wants to talk to you. She has some questions for

you."

"You told her about Carlos?"

"I told you I would."

"How'd she take it?"

"Frankly, she surprised me. She took it very calmly."

By that time, we'd maneuvered through the crowd to a group of women, surrounding a couch, on which Emily Clemson was seated. Joan prodded her way through the ladies, me right behind, until we were in front of Emily.

When she saw us, Emily turned to the women sitting on the couch on both sides of her. She whispered something to them, they got up, and Emily motioned Joan and me into the vacated seats.

The last time I'd met Emily Clemson, she was a bland, easy-to-forget, almost non-person. Nothing about her that you could remember an hour afterwards.

She was different now. Joan had told me her mother was on tranquilizers. Well, maybe yesterday, but not today. Emily Clemson was very much aware, and in control of herself, and her surroundings. She had almost a...I don't know how else to describe it...a commanding presence.

As I sat down, I offered my condolences, Emily nodded her head in acceptance, and then she got right to business.

"So Carl had a son."

It was a statement, not a question.

"He did have an affair," I said, "and there was this boy."

Unlike Joan, Emily had no questions about Carlos Gomez. She was on the hunt for other information.

"Was that my husband's only affair? Or are there others? What can you tell me?" she demanded.

Remember that phrase..."a woman scorned?"

Emily Clemson definitely was that woman right now, and madder than hell about it.

"I only know about this one," I said.

Emily looked at me for a few seconds before speaking again.

"I want to hire you. I want you to find out if Carl has had any other affairs."

I looked at Joan. The surprise on her face mirrored my own. Emily Clemson was no longer the docile wife, a role she'd played for 35 years. She was, instead, a very angry woman who felt betrayed by an unfaithful husband. For just a few seconds, I almost felt sorry for Carl Clemson.

"I can't do that," I told her.

"Why not?"

"Conflict of interest. Your husband has retained me, so I can't work for you, too."

Joan put her hand on her mother's arm.

"Mother, please. None of this is any good. It can't lead to anything good."

For a few seconds, Mrs. Clemson seemed to fight off her daughter's words. Then, the fight went out of her. Anger can take a person only so far. It's a spiking kind of emotion. A strong up, and then a sharp down. Emily was now on the downside of the spike. Her face softened, her body settled back into the couch.

Her two friends, who'd been watching us, came back to the couch, concerned. Joan and I got up and the ladies took our places, each of them putting an arm around Emily's shoulders. Their gestures seemed exactly right as they comforted her.

Joan and I moved away from the couch.

"I'm not sure, now, that I did the right thing," Joan said, "telling my mother about that...affair...and...Carlos Gomez. I reasoned with myself that she had the right to know, that I wouldn't want her to be blindsided if it came out during a police investigation."

"Stop beating yourself up," I told Joan. "You're not to blame for what your father did. And your mother's a grown woman. If she can't handle the dirty laundry, it's not your fault."

Joan smiled, and I could see the tension in her ease a bit.

"That's better," I told her.

She smiled again, then nodded at a short, slightly plump woman dressed in black. The woman was dark-haired and attractive.

"George's wife, Barbara," Joan said.

"I'd like to meet her. Can you introduce me?"

"Of course."

The reason I wanted to meet Barbara Clemson was the same reason I was meeting other members of the Clemson family. To find out anything I could, that might give me a lead as to the writer of the letters, or George's killer. Yes, I know I've been telling you Carlos Gomez is a contender on both of those deals, but obviously, he's not a one hundred per cent certainty. So, on to Barbara Clemson.

Joan made the introductions and then left us.

I offered my condolences.

"Thank you," Barbara said, staring at me, obviously trying to place who I was in this roomful of mourners. Then it came to her.

"You're the private detective my father-in-law hired to find out who is writing those threatening letters to him."

"That's right," I confirmed.

"Well, when you find that person, please thank him for me," Barbara said harshly.

Surprise. Another family fan of Carl Clemson's.

"I know Carl made life pretty rough for your husband," I said. "I'm sorry."

"Rough is not the right word for it," Barbara said sadly. "A phrase like 'hell on earth,' would be more appropriate."

She paused for a moment, then continued, her face and voice reflecting her anger.

"George had to go to a therapist five times a week, Monday through Friday, for the last year. The pressure he felt from his father was so bad, he needed to see a psychiatrist every day! That, Mr. Jonas, is no way to live."

What am I supposed to answer to a statement like that? You have any ideas? I didn't, so I went back to my original game plan.

"I'd like to talk with you some more, Mrs. Clemson," I said. "I need more information."

And then I played the best card I had.

"Information that could help me, and help the police, to find your husband's,,,to find who is responsible."

Barbara sighed and sagged, then nodded.

"We're in the book," she told me. "Encino."

I couldn't help noticing her saying, 'we're' in the book. Not, 'I'm' in the book. That would take some time, I knew. It was the same when my Vera died. Took me almost a year to stop saying, 'we,' and moving over to 'I.' Just another example of not letting go of something that had been good.

Barbara Clemson and I parted, and Joan was at my side again.

"You need to talk to Stanley. Please."

"Okay. Where is he?"

Joan led me across the living room, into the hall, and then in to the same room where Emily Clemson and I had first met. It was crowded in here, too, but not as jammed as the living room. Joan cut through the crowd, exchanging nods with several people. I followed.

We reached a set of French doors, Joan opened one of them, and we went out, on to a large balcony. Stanley was standing by the rail. My first look at him confirmed for me what Joan had said. Stanley was in a very uptight state. I know that's not much of a medical description, but it was clear that he was under a lot of pressure.

"Stanley," Joan greeted her brother, coming close to him and giving him a soft kiss on the cheek.

Stanley stared at me. I don't know why, but my being there seemed to frighten him.

"What is he doing here?" he demanded.

"I asked him to come," Joan told him.

"And I wanted to pay my respects," I said. "I'm sorry for what happened to your brother."

Stanley shook his head.

"You don't know anything about what happened," he shouted, "You don't know anything."

I jumped in, to take advantage of the opening he'd given me.

"I guess I don't," I offered, "so why don't you tell me what happened."

"How can I tell you anything?" Stanley shouted. "I wasn't there! So how can I tell you anything?"

And then he pushed Joan away and ran back inside.

I looked at Joan.

"What was that all about? Do you have any idea?"

"No," she answered. "See what I mean? About the way he's acting? I don't understand what's going on with him, but I'm scared."

I tried to comfort her.

"Look. I'll try to see him in a day or two. When he's calmed down. I'm sure he'll be alright."

"God, I hope so."

Now, Carl Clemson came out to the balcony. He glared at me.

"We have to talk," he said. He looked at Joan. "Alone," he added.

Joan looked at her father, then at me, gave a little nod and walked back inside.

Clemson wasted no time ramming into me.

"What the hell are you doing? Checking into my past? And telling my family about Maria Gomez and that bastard son of hers?"

"That 'bastard son' of hers, is your bastard," I shot back.

"Not that I know of," Carl said. "I wasn't the only man that slut slept with!"

So that was going to be the official line, if or when this information came out. Carl would admit to the infidelity, but claim Carlos wasn't his. That the woman was sleeping around. I wondered if Carl had conferred with his downtown lawyers on that one, or figured it out for himself. Either way, it was neat.

"You really believe that line of shit?" I asked.

Carl looked at me, surprised I guess, at how I was giving it back to him. Not too many people did. But not too many people had the benefit of their own fathers being like Carl. I had plenty of experience for these nose-to-nose encounters, thanks, or no thanks, to my old man.

"You're fired," Carl said. "You don't work for me anymore. Is that clear?"

"Just when it's getting interesting?" I couldn't help asking sarcastically.

"Cut the shit, Jonas, or you'll be sorry," Clemson said. "Very sorry."

He nodded toward the house.

"You see who's in there tonight? I can squash you like any other bug that bothers me. Get your license cancelled any time. Understand?"

Clemson didn't wait for an answer, but instead, he turned and went back inside.

And now, I was really pissed!

It wasn't like I'd never been talked to like that before. Threatened before. Being a cop means being threatened almost every day. Especially when you're in Homicide.

But this time around, I took it more personally. Don't know why, exactly. Maybe because I liked Joan Clemson? Probably.

And maybe, too, because I never, when I was a cop, and since I've been a private investigator, I never liked leaving a case that wasn't finished. Just filing it away. Note that I didn't say, 'solved.' I said, 'finished.' I'd filed plenty of unsolved cases. But I was the one who decided when to file them.

And I wasn't ready to file this one yet! I wasn't going to stop. Just because Clemson had fired me. So he wasn't paying me anymore? Hey, it wouldn't be the first time I'd worked for nothing.

Chapter Twenty

For the next two days, things were all mixed up in my head. Lots of loose thoughts. Connected in some way. Only I couldn't figure out how.

Question: how come Emily Clemson, obedient and docile all these years, got so tough and determined when she found out Carl had fathered a son out of wedlock?

Question: was there anything more than friendship between Bill Schlesinger and Emily Clemson? He'd spoken so fondly of her. And she of him.

And okay, here was the really bugging question. Could George Clemson have been the product of a union between…Emily Clemson and Bill Schlesinger?

Hah! You didn't see that one coming, did you? Well, chew on this.

George and Bill Schlesinger were about the same size and build. Slender. About five eight or nine. They had similar light skin coloring, hair texture, and light brown hair. Since Emily also was slight in stature, and blond, George was the kind of offspring you'd expect from Emily and Bill.

What did any of this have to do with the threatening letters Carl Clemson was getting? Or with the killing of George Clemson?

Damned if I knew. But I also knew from past experience, that when I started getting questions like these bouncing around in my head, I needed to get answers. Because it was those answers that would lead me to solving this case.

And that's why I was parking in front of Bill Schlesinger's house again. I'd called him earlier and asked if we could meet. He'd agreed, although he didn't sound too happy about it.

"I'd hoped I'd seen the last of you," Schlesinger told me when we were seated in his living room. "You make me remember things I don't want to think about."

"Sorry about that, but I've got more questions, and I'm hoping you can give me the answers."

"Like?"

"Like…was George Clemson your and Emily's son? Your son. Not Carl's."

Ever hear the expression 'his jaw dropped?'

Schlesinger's sure did. He stared at me, but I kept my mouth shut. I figured he'd eventually talk – and he did.

"That's the dumbest thing I ever heard. How did you ever come up with an idea like that?"

"Not so dumb, as I see it," I said. And then I went on to tell Schlesinger my thinking. About how fondly he had spoken of Emily. And Emily of him. And about the physical resemblance George had to Emily and him. Rather than to Carl Clemson.

Schlesinger shook his head.

"You're pretty damned observant. I'll give you that, But you're way off base," he told me.

Only there was something in the way he answered, how he avoided looking directly at me, that tipped me. I was sure I was hitting some sort of a mark, even if it wasn't exactly the right one. So, I pushed harder.

"Suppose I ask Emily Clemson the same question?"

Schlesinger jerked upright in his seat and pointed his finger at me.

"Don't you dare!" he shouted.

He held that finger out at me for emphasis until, with a sigh, he let his hand fall back into his lap. He licked his lips, shook his head, took a deep breath and started talking.

"You have to understand some things. I'll tell you about them, but then, God, I hope you'll walk away from it. There's been enough anguish and tears. Nothing will be gained by opening it all up again."

He stopped to take another deep breath.

"Emily and I never had an affair. We never slept together. Not even once. I'll swear to that, and mean it, on my parents' graves. We were very fond of each other. But it was as friends, and that's all. There is absolutely no way that George could have been my son."

He stopped again and stared at me, obviously finding it hard to say what was coming next.

"But George also – was not – Carl's son. Not biologically, that is."

This time, it was me with the dropped jaw.

"Okay," I asked when I recovered. "So, who's son was

George?"

Schlesinger folded and unfolded his hands several times. Then, he leaned toward me for emphasis.

"What I'm going to tell you now, is something Emily told me, and made me swear I'd never tell anyone. I think the only reason she told me, was because she could not keep it to herself. The emotional pressure was too great."

Schlesinger paused again, and I felt like leaning over and pulling the words out of his mouth. But I didn't say anything, and eventually he started talking.

"As I've told you before, Emily was miserable when Carl moved her down here. I'm sure that by now, she's more...polished. But then, she was just a sweet girl from a small town and she needed some attention. Someone caring about her.

"But Carl was into building the business. Working 14, 16 hours a day. He and I both did. Only I was single. Carl, of course, wasn't. But he acted like he was. No room in that schedule for Emily.

"There was a pharmacist, at the drug store the Clemsons went to. And he was...attentive and friendly to Emily, whenever she went in there. Giving her advice on which brands to buy. What the best price deals were.

"And they talked. Just chatting. Everyday stuff. But, it was someone paying attention to Emily. And that was important.

"In retrospect," Emily told me, "she sort of knew that Richard...that was his name, Richard Bellows...was a charmer. But to Emily at that time, sad, lonely, you name it, Richard at least was someone who talked to her. Listened to her.

"They slept together only once. Richard showed up, unexpectedly, one evening. Emily, in one of her chats with Richard, had mentioned that Carl was out of town on a buying trip. Did she say that on purpose? Or was it just an innocent comment? Emily didn't know herself. Regardless, with Carl away, Emily was feeling especially down."

"And there was Richard," I said.

"And there was Richard," Schlesinger answered. "And you can fill in the rest."

"What happened when Emily found out she was pregnant?" I asked. "Did she go to Bellows? Did she think about an abortion?"

Schlesinger laughed, only there was no humor in it.

"By the time Emily realized she was pregnant, Bellows was gone. Left Los Angeles for places unknown. As for an abortion, remember, this was the early 1960's. Not as easy, then, as it is today. Especially for someone as insecure and needy as Emily was at that time in her life."

"So, what did she do?"

"She went to Carl. To tell him. To beg his forgiveness. Hardest thing in the world she ever did, she told me.

"She expected Carl would make her get an abortion, and she was ready for that. But Carl forgave her."

"He forgave her?" I echoed, surprised. "That's kind of out of character for Clemson, isn't it?"

"Yes it is," Schlesinger agreed. "But what was in character for Carl, coldhearted sonofabitch that he was, and is, was that he came up with a plan to take advantage of Emily's pregnancy.

"You see, Emily and Carl had been trying, for over a year, to have a child. After a while, they went and had some tests. This was way before the kind of stuff they're doing nowadays, of course.

"Emily tested fine. No problems with her. But the tests showed that Carl had a weak sperm count. He could father children, the doctors told him, but he just had to be patient."

"But Carl was impatient," I anticipated, "and along comes Emily, now, with one already cooking."

Schlesinger nodded.

"You have it right. Carl told Emily that no one had to know about Richard Bellows. He'd already left town, Emily had never had a chance to tell Bellows he had impregnated her, and Carl said he would claim the fatherhood.

"Of course, Carl being Carl, he also pointed out to Emily, that he was rescuing her from disgrace. That he had the right to divorce her. He ground her down real good.

"She agreed to his conditions, which were, to keep quiet and to acknowledge the baby as being Carl's and hers. Carl would get that child he wanted so badly, and Emily would keep her honor, and her marriage. No one would ever know.

"And that's the way it was, except that Emily had to share that secret, so she told me. But we never spoke of it after that one time, and shortly afterwards, Carl bought me out of our partnership, and he forbade Emily from being in contact with me. I think, though I can't prove it, that he suspected I knew the truth, so he was determined to cut Emily off from me."

Schlesinger fished in his pocket, took out a handkerchief and wiped his face.

"Now that you know," he asked me, "what are you going to do with the information?"

Chapter Twenty-One

What am I going to do with the information, Schlesinger had asked me.

I didn't have an answer for him, when he asked. And now, as I headed back to my car, I still didn't know. I decided that, for now, I'd let this bombshell of a fact just stir around in my head, along with all of the other thoughts in my confused mind.

Back in my car, I turned on my pager. I'd shut it off for the meeting because I didn't want any interruptions. Who says we're not masters of our destiny?

There was one page, from Rose. I called her.

"It's been an hour since I paged you. Why didn't you call me right away?" she demanded.

What was that about mastering our destiny?

"What's so important?" I asked.

"Charlie Black called. They have Carlos Gomez. Charlie said to let you know, in case you wanted to watch the interrogation. They are at the stationhouse now."

I was there in twenty minutes. Charlie had left word with the desk sergeant, and he passed me through to Homicide, where the administrative assistant told me which observation room to go to.

Manny Soto and an assistant district attorney, Miles Groverman, were in the room. Miles and I had worked several cases together. He was a capable prosecutor.

"What are you doing here?" Soto demanded. "No civilians allowed in here."

"And hello to you, too, Manny," I said putting on a full smile. "Come on, bend a little. Hell, I'm the one who found out about Gomez. I'm sure Charlie told you that."

Miles came to my rescue.

"No reason Will can't be here, Manny. No problem, as far as I'm concerned."

Manny and I stared at each other for a few seconds, then he shrugged.

"Just stay out of the way," he warned, having to get in the last word.

"Sure," I said, not letting him do so. Male hormones at work, huh?

The three of us turned toward the one-way mirror. I took a good look at Carlos Gomez. And what I saw was a definite resemblance to Carl Clemson. Although it was hard to tell, because he was sitting down, Gomez looked to be about six feet tall, which is big for a Mexican man. He was thin, not as broad as Carl, but he had the same shape face, the same slightly long and straight nose. Put the two of them together, and it wouldn't be hard to believe they were conceived by a white father and a Mexican mother.

Charlie and Tom were just finishing up. When a uniform came in to stand guard, they left Gomez, his hands cuffed to the table.

The two came into the observation room. Charlie nodded to me, then spoke to Groverman.

"Well?"

"You didn't get much," Groverman said. "You know that."

"Enough to hold him over, until we check out his alibi about where he was the night Clemson was killed?" Tom asked

Groverman gave that some thought.

"Well, he's been read his rights. The father-son angle does give us some basis for considering motive. He hasn't asked for a lawyer." He looked at his watch. "Okay, you can keep him for the full twenty four hours, up until noon tomorrow. But then you have to let him go, or charge him, and give him an opportunity to be represented by counsel."

Charlie nodded.

"That's time enough for us to check out his alibi," he said.

Later, Charlie and I were having coffee in the stationhouse as he brought me up to date.

"We picked Gomez up around twelve, when he came back to his dump of a house."

"Any problem bringing him in?"

"Nah. He knows the drill. He's got a pretty fair sized jacket."

"What's in it?"

"A couple of battery and assault charges. He's also been picked up three times for suspected drug dealing. Couldn't nail him, though, and even if it had been possible, he's smalltime. Not a major pusher, or anything close to that."

"A user?"

"Doesn't look like he's using now, but judging by the scars, he's been there."

"What's he say about the homicide? Or the letters?"

"Claims he doesn't know anything about either one, Says he was in Long Beach all last week. Shacking up with a new broad he met, when George was killed. Tom's on his way to Long Beach now, to interview her. Gomez gave us her address.

"As for the letters, Gomez says he doesn't have a computer. And doesn't even know how to use one, A little hard to believe that last part, but that's what he claims. But anyway, even if that's true, it doesn't let him off the hook. He could've had someone else do them for him. Maybe even his Long Beach lady friend. Tom's checking that angle out, too."

"Okay, what about the resemblance between Gomez and Carl Clemson? Did you see it?"

Charlie nodded.

"Yeah, I saw it. And anyway, when I asked him, Gomez acknowledged Clemson was his father. And he also said that, as he put it, 'I hate the fucking bastard.' He also admitted that every once in a while, he thought about going to Carl and demanding some money, to keep quiet about who he is. But he said he never did that."

"Why not?"

"He says he figured Clemson would blow him off. Like he did to his mother. What with all his connections and all."

I remembered the line Clemson had fed me, when I first confronted him about Maria Gomez and her baby. 'I wasn't the only man that slut slept with.' And I had to admit that Carlos was probably right.

Chapter Twenty-Two

I'd been trying to see Stanley Clemson ever since the wake at his parent's home, when Joan and I talked to him on the balcony. He hadn't returned my calls, and it was clear that he was avoiding me.

Time to close the loop on that one, so when I left Charlie, I drove directly to Stanley's townhome in Woodland Hills. Joan had given me the address. I planned to drop in on Stanley, unannounced. It was 7:30 PM and I was hoping he'd be home.

Stanley lived in a garden townhome complex, surrounded by a security fence, with access through a pedestrian gate. You had to buzz the unit you were visiting, and then that party would open the gate. I didn't want to alert Stanley that I was coming to see him, so I didn't want to buzz him. I could have buzzed another unit and tried to talk my way through the gate...you know... got a pizza for...but why bother? There was an easier way.

I walked over to the driveway gate of the complex and waited for a car to show up. There's always plenty of in and out traffic at a place like this between 6 and 8 PM.

In a couple of minutes, a car did drive up, the gate opened, and the driver went in. After the car was out of sight, I walked in, just as the gate was swinging shut.

Ah, the safety of a security fence.

As I approached Stanley's unit, I could see lights on inside. Good. So he probably was home. Either that, or he had one of those security systems that turned the lights on when it started getting dark.

He was home. After I rang the bell, I heard him come to the door and saw the visitor peephole open. I smiled my best. It didn't help.

"What do you want?" Stanley asked, through the closed door.

"To come inside and talk to you," I answered. "Come on, Stanley, you know you're going to have to talk to me. Let's do it now, and get it over with."

"I don't have to talk to you. You're not the police."

"Your sister says she wants you to talk to me. You know she wants that, Stanley. You know Joan cares."

I'd said the right thing. Stanley unlocked the door, opened it, and stepped aside to let me in. Then I followed him into his living room and we sat down.

If Carl Clemson's illegitimate son, Carlos, was hard and mean, in contrast Stanley was soft and nervous. Emphasis on nervous. He looked like hell. He was bent over, in what looked to me like a defensive posture, his shoulders hunched, like he was waiting to ward off some kind of a blow.

"What's going on, Stanley?" I asked, keeping my voice soft and friendly. "You look…worried. What is it?"

Stanley bit his lip and straightened up in his chair.

"I don't know what you mean. And I don't know why you're here. I have nothing to tell you."

I sat back in my seat, crossed my legs and made myself look perfectly at ease. I wanted Stanley to feel I wasn't pushing.

"You're probably right," I agreed. "You probably don't have anything to tell me. It's just that, ever since this business started with your father getting those letters, and now, with…what happened to George, I've been talking to all the members of the family, trying to figure out who might be behind these things. Who might want to do harm to your father, or to George."

"I don't know of anyone," Stanley mumbled, looking down at his hands in his lap.

"No one at all who might be mad at your father? We all know he's not an easy man to get along with. To do business with."

"No one," was all that Stanley gave me back.

Something was wrong here. I'd been with Stanley and George before, and at the time, neither of them was bashful about knocking Carl. So, why the clam up by Stanley, now? It didn't make sense.

"Come on, Stanley," I coaxed, "you must know of someone who'd like to take a swing at your father. Maybe even go so far as to…kill George, as a way of getting at your father?

"I don't know anything about what happened to George!" Stanley shouted at me. "I wasn't there, remember?"

What I remembered was, seeing Stanley's car, along with Carl's and George's, as the only cars in the parking lot the last time I'd gone to Clemson Automotive. I'd reasoned, then, that the owners were always the last to leave. A reasonable assumption, I thought.

So, why hadn't Stanley been there when George was killed? I wanted to know more about that.

"If you weren't there that night, then where were you?"

"I was working out. At my gym. That's where I was."

"What gym is that?"

"Don't you believe me?"

"Sure. So, what gym is it?"

"WorkOuts."

"Which one?" WorkOuts was a chain operation, I knew.

"The one on DeSoto. North of Parthenia."

"Okay,"

I decided to keep quiet, and to just stare at Stanley. It was my experience that when nervous, scared people are stared at, silently, they often can't stand it, and they start to ramble, come out with all sorts of useful information.

No such luck this time, though. Stanley looked at me, the anxiety clear on his face.

"I'd like you to leave," he said. "Please," he added, his voice soft and uncertain.

A thought ran through my mind. Could Stanley have killed George? Wow! Was that one out in left field! Still, it might explain why the guy was so nervous. He'd been weak before George was killed. But now, he was a wreck. Maybe the result of pressure brought on by his killing George? A real long shot here. I doubted it. But still…

I got up.

"Thanks for seeing me, Stanley." I held out my hand, with my card. "And if there is anything else you can think of, I'd sure appreciate a call. Okay?"

Stanley took the card like it was covered with a fatal strain of some virus. He didn't answer me, but instead, he turned and walked toward the front door, to let me out.

When I got home, I started to call Lu in Cleveland, but then I realized that since it was 8:30 here in Los Angeles, that made it 11:30 there. Too late to call.

A couple of minutes later, as I was deciding between a lasagna dinner in the freezer, or ordering a pizza from Uncle Ernie's, the phone rang.

It was Joan Clemson.

"Stanley called me," she said. "I gather it wasn't much of a meeting, except to upset Stanley even more?"

I recapped my conversation with Stanley, and then I added, "I don't know what's going on, Joan. But something very heavy is bothering your brother. Tearing him up. I couldn't get through to him. Maybe you can?"

"I've tried, but he's just as non-responsive with me as he was with you. I'm very worried about him."

There were a couple of things that I had to tell Joan, and now was as good a time as any.

I said, "I haven't had a chance to talk to you since the wake, and I need to give you some information."

"Oh? What would that be?"

"First, your father's fired me. Told me to stop working on the case."

"Fired you? Why? You've been more effective than all the police put together. You're the one who found Carlos Gomez, for goodness sake."

"That's exactly why he fired me. He didn't appreciate my bringing up that part of his past life. In fact, he was madder than hell about it."

"Then I want to hire you," Joan said. "I want to hire you to continue your investigation."

"Hey, thanks for the vote of confidence. Only, you don't have to hire me. I've hired myself."

"I don't understand."

"Simple enough. I'm too much into this investigation to walk away from it. Not my style. Not the way I operate. I'm continuing, whether or not your father likes it."

I didn't mention to Joan her father's threat to squash me like some kind of bug. No need to worry her about that. And I wasn't going to worry about it, either. At least, not until something squashable started happening.

"Thank you, Will," Joan said. "I...really appreciate what you are doing."

"It's okay," I told her. "And there's something else I want to tell you. The police have found Carlos Gomez."

"Do you know where he is, Will? I want to meet him."

"I don't know how good an idea that is," I told her. "I don't think you'll like what you meet."

"Will, he's my half brother. I need to meet him. Please. You have to help me in this."

"Look," I said, "he's in custody tonight. The police are checking out his alibi, about where he was, when George was…killed, Damn it Joan! He's a suspect in your brother's murder. How can you want to see him?"

"Because he's…family. I…can't explain it any better than that."

"Okay," I agreed reluctantly.

"When?"

"It depends on what happens by noon tomorrow. If the alibi he's given the police doesn't hold up, then they'll arrest him, charge him and have him arraigned. And it might be a few days until I can get you in to see him.

"If his alibi does hold up, he'll be let go tomorrow afternoon,"

"And then you'll take me to see him?"

"Yes."

"Will," Joan said, "thank you. I'm really grateful."

After Joan hung up, the only thing left to do, was to eat.

The lasagna won my vote.

Chapter Twenty-Three

The next day, I went to the WorkOuts on DeSoto in Northridge. In the all-white and chrome reception area, I was greeted by a cover girl blond with shoulder length hair, eighty-seven gleaming teeth, and skin that had never known a zits.

"May I help you?" she smiled, but I knew what she was really thinking. If this old guy joins, the average age of the membership will go up by 25 years. Ever notice how most of the members of these muscle mania mansions are perpetually in their twenties?

Every once in a while, I sort of impersonate the police officer I used to be. I say, "sort of," because as a private investigator, I'm not supposed to do things like that. But if I do it carefully enough, no problem, and it does make it easier to get information I need, from people who might otherwise not give it to me.

Shall I demonstrate?

I wanted two pieces of information from this House of Hormones. The name of Stanley Clemson's trainer, and to confirm that Stanley was here, as he claimed he was, at the time and on the night that George was killed.

"I need to talk to the manager, about a homicide I'm investigating," I told Beautiful Blond.

See? I didn't say I was a cop investigating a homicide. Just that I was investigating a homicide. I am so slick!

Beautiful Blond lost her smile when I mentioned the H word. She quickly dialed a number on her white phone and said something into the mouthpiece. I wondered what it would be like to be a mouthpiece, with those gorgeous lips caressing…

Quicker than you could say tight buns, a male version of the receptionist came out to see me. He was also blond, a little shorter than me, had even more teeth than Beautiful Blond, was half my age, and he looked like he'd just been poured into his workout outfit. I hated him. Nah. No hatred. Some jealousy, maybe. Maybe?

"Detective…?" Male Blond said, "I'm Ray Royal, the day manager. Can I help you?"

Ray Royal?

I kid you not. That was his name. I can't swear he was born with it. But with Hollywood just a freeway away, he had to be prepared for that next casting call.

"Ray Royal, starring in Flex Those Abs."

"Will Jonas," I said.

Was I clever? Please notice I didn't say "Detective Will Jonas." No siree. Of course, I didn't deny that he called me a detective, but he said it, not me.

Enough inside tricks of the trade for today. On with the tail.

"I need to check whether one of your members really was here," I said, "when he claims he was working out with his personal trainer."

"What's the member's name?"

"Stanley Clemson."

"Let's take a look at the personal trainer appointment schedule," Ray Royal said, walking behind the receptionist's desk. "What night are we talking about?"

"Last Wednesday night. Sometime between five and eight ought to cover it."

The manager took a couple of minutes to go through the records, then he reported to me.

"Mr. Clemson works out with Vincent. His regular workout night is Tuesday, from seven to eight pm. And last week, that's when he was here. Tuesday. Not Wednesday."

"You're sure?"

"Yes. Of course, our clients do change appointments, but when this happens, our trainers know they have to make the change in the appointment book on the computer. It's the basis of our billing system. And last week, Mr. Clemson was here on Tuesday, not Wednesday, for his weekly appointment. Would you like me to get Vincent out here to confirm?"

"If you could. Just to make sure."

Ray picked up the reception desk phone, dialed a number and then said something to someone. A minute later, Vincent came out. Same mold as Ray, I wasn't surprised to see.

Ray explained the situation to Vincent, who also checked the appointment book.

"That's right," he told me. "Mr. Clemson was here last Tuesday night, for his regular appointment. We're very careful about having the right information in here. I would definitely remember if I'd had to change the appointment entry. And I didn't have to."

After Vincent went back inside to show whatever client he had back there how to make a bigger bicep, Ray Royal's curiosity got the better of him

"I hope...I mean, there isn't any problem with Mr. Clemson, is there?"

"No," I assured him. "And thank you for your help."

I turned to Beautiful Blond.

"You got great teeth," I told her, on my way out.

She loved it.

"Thank you," she called after me, flashing her widest smile.

Maybe it was ninety-seven teeth?

Outside, I sat in my car and thought about what I'd just learned.

Stanley Clemson had lied to me, when he said he'd been here, at WorkOut, on Wednesday night, the night George was killed.

I definitely had to do some more digging to find out where Stanley was that night.

Chapter Twenty-Four

Later that day, I was doing something I didn't want to do, but I had no choice. Joan Clemson had made me promise that I'd take her to meet Carlos Gomez, and here we were, in my car, on the way to his house.

I'd checked with Charlie earlier in the day. Tom Gorcey had met with the woman in Long Beach, and she'd confirmed that Carlos Gomez was with her last week, including Wednesday night, when George Clemson was shot and killed. So, Gomez was telling the truth on that score, and shortly before noon, he'd been released from custody.

But even if he was clear of the killing of George Clemson, Gomez wasn't your everyday law-abiding citizen, and I wasn't happy about taking Joan to meet him.

"You still sure you want to do this?" I asked her.

"Yes."

Joan was staring straight ahead, her hands in her lap, her fingers fidgeting with one of her rings, turning the ring around and around.

"What are you looking for?" I argued. "Some sort of a relationship with a person you don't know at all? Have nothing in common with?"

"But we do have something in common. The same father."

"From what I know about Gomez, I don't think that means very much to him."

We arrived at the Gomez house and I parked in front of it.

"This is it," I told Joan.

We sat in the car. Joan stared at the dilapidated heap Gomez called home. She took a deep breath and opened her door

"Let's go, please."

We got out of the car and walked through the yard, up the two-step porch, to the front door.

I knocked on it, and after a few beats, it opened.

Carlos Gomez, in sorry jeans and a t-shirt that hadn't seen the inside of a washing machine for a while, stared at us.

"Yeah?" he asked.

Although I knew who he was, Gomez didn't have a clue who I was. I'd seen him through the one-way mirror at the stationhouse, but he'd never seen me.

"I'm Will Jonas, I said. "I left you that note on my card?"

"You another cop?" he asked harshly. "You guys got nothing better to do than to hassle me?"

"I'm not a cop. I'm a private investigator."

"You used to be a cop. It's all over you."

He turned to Joan.

"You a cop, too? You don't look like no cop."

"I'm...your sister," Joan said hesitantly, softly.

Carlos stared at her.

"My sister? What do you mean?"

"Your father...is also...my father...Carl Clemson?"

It took a few seconds for that to sink in, but when it did, Carlos's anger was clear on his face and in his voice.

"Hey, Lady, maybe he's your father, but he don't mean jackshit to me! What the fuck are you doing here?"

"I wanted to meet you. To see you. To...talk with you," Joan pleaded.

"It's too late for that! I don't wanna talk to you. Now, get the hell out of here!"

"Please..." Joan said, taking a step toward Carlos.

"Don't you understand fuckin' English? Get outta here! Now!"

Gomez looked ready to take a swing at Joan and I tensed, ready to step in between them.

But Joan stepped back.

"I'm...sorry...you...won't talk to me. I'm not like my father. Believe me. I do want to get to know you."

"Go peddle that shit somewhere else. I don't wanna talk to you. Or get to know you."

Gomez stepped back and slammed the door shut. Joan stood there, staring at the door.

I waited a few seconds. Then I took hold of her arm.

"Come on," I said to her, gently. "It's no use."

Joan said nothing, but she let me walk her back to my car.

As I drove away, Joan looked at Carlos's house. Then she turned to me.

"You were right, of course," she said, her voice soft and sad.

Then she banged the palm of her hand against the dashboard

in front of her.

"That sonofabitch!" she yelled. "That sonofabitch!"

"Joan," I tried to reason with her, "after all this time, it would be hard for Carlos to accept anyone connected with your family."

"I don't mean him," Joan snapped. "I mean my father. He's the sonofabitch who's made this happen. Someone should have killed my father, instead of poor George!"

Chapter Twenty-Five

When I walked into my office the next morning, Rose held a finger to her lips and waived me over to her desk.

"You've got someone in there. I tried to keep him out here, but I couldn't stop him."

"Who is it?"

"He told me he was Detective Manny Soto. I'm sorry. I tried to stop him."

"It's okay, Rose," I assured her.

I left Rose and went into my office. Soto was on my side of the desk, pawing through my papers.

"What the hell are you doing," I snarled at him. "What's there is none of your business!"

Soto took his time putting down the papers he was holding, which irritated me even more. He saw that, and he smiled, which...well, you get the idea.

"Gee," he said, "You'd think there was something confidential here. Maybe something you're not supposed to be doing?"

I walked up close to him. Soto was a good five inches shorter than me. I wouldn't have hit him, of course. Not a good idea to hit cops. But my size backed him off a little, and he moved around to the visitor's side of my desk.

"Why are you here, Manny? What do you want?"

"It isn't what I want," Soto shot back at me. "It's what Carl Clemson doesn't want."

"What's that?" I asked, although I already knew the answer.

"I'll put it in simple words that even you can understand. Mr. Clemson fired you from this case, remember? He thinks maybe you've forgotten, because you keep going around, talking to people connected with it. And he doesn't want that. He wants you off the case, like he told you in the first place."

"I didn't know you were on Clemson's payroll, Manny. I thought you worked for the City, same as most cops."

"Cut the crap," Soto bristled. "I'm doing this because the Chief, as in Chief of Police, told me to do it. Clemson called him, complaining about you. You don't stop, he'll be calling the mayor, next. You want that?"

It figured. This would be the way Clemson would operate. Go

straight to the top brass to get done what you wanted done.

So what?

"It's still a free country, Manny. And besides, Joan Clemsons' hired me to continue working on the case."

Well, that wasn't quite true. She'd wanted to hire me, but I'd told her it wasn't necessary, that I was going to continue on my own. Same thing, though, if you bend the words a bit.

Soto stared at me for a few seconds, and by the look on his face, I knew he had some other bad news for me, something he was happy to deliver.

"All that may be so," he said, "but you should keep one thing in mind."

He pointed at my framed private investigator's license hanging on the wall behind my desk.

"That license you got there, to be a private investigator? It's issued by the City of Los Angeles. And what the City issues, it can pull. Revoke. Could happen to you. Happens to private dicks all the time."

The threat to take away my license had to be coming straight from what Clemson wanted. Part of the bug squashing he'd threatened me with, when we argued at George's wake.

Well, I'd worry about the license deal at some point in the future. Even for Clemson, the mayor or anybody else, pulling a PI's license had to start with a hearing. And we were nowhere near that point yet.

"Okay," I told Soto. "You've given me Clemson's message. Done your errand for today. Now, get out of my office. I've got things to do."

The main thing I had to do, was to meet Barbara Clemson at three o'clock that afternoon, at her home in Encino. The house was up in the hills, south of Ventura Boulevard, in an area called Lake Encino. Cheap homes in Lake Encino were those price-tagged for sale at about $750,000, and many were worth a million plus.

A maid showed me into a decorator-perfect living room, and said Mrs. Clemson would be with me in a few minutes. She was true to her word. Just a short wait, and then Barbara came in.

The days since the funeral had been good to her. She looked much calmer. Maybe, too, it was the light colored skirt and blouse she was wearing. The combination looked better on her than the black dress she wore at the funeral.

"Mr. Jonas," she greeted me. "Can I get you anything? Coffee? Tea?"

"Thanks, but nothing right now."

I sat down at one end of a couch, and Barbara sat at the other end.

"How can I help you?" she asked.

"I hope...you won't mind if I ask you some questions about your husband. It's necessary, I assure you."

"I suspect your questions won't be any different than those the police asked, so go ahead," she said, giving me an encouraging nod.

'I'm sure they asked you this one," I started. "Did your husband have any enemies? Anyone who might have reason to hurt George?"

Barbara shook her head.

"My husband was a sweet, gentle man. He never hurt anyone. He was far too timid for that. No, I can't think of any enemies he might have developed. In business, or otherwise."

Before I could ask my next question, Barbara leaned toward me and spat out her next words.

"It was Carl who made enemies, Mr. Jonas. He's the one who should have been killed!"

She shook her head again.

"You know something? I'd be tempted, myself, to shoot Carl, for how miserable he made George."

"It was pretty bad, huh?"

"Bad doesn't describe it. That man destroyed his son. Every day. He picked on him. Pressured him, so that George would come home a wreck. The last several weeks before he...died...George was so terribly depressed. He was going to Dr. Kliegman for a session every day."

"Did they help?"

"Some. But the good the psychiatrist accomplished would get washed away, every time something new came along. Like that latest maneuver by Carl. It troubled George terribly."

"What maneuver do you mean?"

"Carl's plan for turning Clemson Automotive around. The company was having some problems, you see. Cash flow problems, George told me. And Carl decided to put in a hard cost cutting program. Cut staff and things like that. It also was Carl's idea to approach Acme and open discussions for Acme to acquire Clemson Automotive."

"Sounds like the right thing to do," I said.

"Oh, there is no arguing that. But the terrible thing is, Carl went ahead with all of that – the cost cutting program and the discussions with Acme – without ever telling George, or Stanley. As a result, George was more and more depressed. He felt so…worthless at Clemson Automotive."

"I'll ask you the obvious," I said. "Did George ever try to talk to his father about those problems? And did he ever tell him it had gotten so bad, he had to see a psychiatrist?"

Barbara looked at me in disbelief.

"Do you honestly think it's ever possible to talk to Carl about the way he runs things? And as for Dr. Kliegman, the last thing George wanted his father to know, was that he was seeing a psychiatrist. In George's view, and I believe he was right, the only thing Carl would do in response, is use that knowledge to further browbeat him."

The lady had a point.

Chapter Twenty-Six

I had no plans to see Charlie Black the next day, but see him I did. More specifically, I saw him the next night.

It was late. After ten o'clock. I was in my knock-around-the-house sweats, watching NYPD Blue. Seeing how the really good cops, like Andy Sipowicz and Bobby Simone solved their cases in 48 minutes.

My phone rang. I didn't want to pick it up. Sipowicz and Simone were questioning a murder suspect, and I was learning all kinds of new things about how to do an interrogation.

But when the damn thing wouldn't stop ringing, I finally did answer it. Anyway, Andy and Bobby had just taken a break for a commercial, so I figured I could, too.

"I sure wouldn't want to be one of Carl Clemson's sons," Charlie said, when I picked up the receiver.

"Why's that?"

"Because they keep getting knocked off."

"What! You mean Stanley Clemson's been killed?"

"Na. Carlos Gomez. Wanna see the beautiful corpse?"

A half hour later, I reached the home of the late Carlos Gomez. The house and grounds were surrounded by the usual scene-of-the-crime yellow tape. When I got out of my car, I saw the old man from next door, standing with the other looky-loo neighbors. He waived to me, and I waived back.

On the phone, in answer to my question, Charlie had told me Manny Soto was out of town, so there'd be no problem with my showing up.

The uniform at the front gate had my name on his list, and after checking, he told me to go in. I said hello to Charlie and then looked at Gomez.

He was lying in the middle of the floor in what passed for a living room. No carpet or rug. Just Carlos, a beat up wood floor, and a ring of blood surrounding his head like a halo.

I looked around the room. There wasn't much furniture unless you counted the empty pizza boxes and beer cans all over the place.

"I guess the maid didn't get in on her regular day this week," Charlie said as he watched me check out the room.

"And she didn't do the windows, either," I said.

"Doesn't make a rat's ass of difference, anymore." Charlie nodded toward Gomez's body. "Interesting development,"

"You think so?" I asked.

"Well, he is, or was, another offspring of our popular Carl Clemson."

"Yeah, but Clemson never recognized Gomez as his son. Never had any contact with him."

"Killers can have their own ideas about relationships," Charlie said. "Maybe this one's just out to kill all of Clemson's sons, recognized or not."

"There've been stranger things," I agreed. "You going to move along those lines?"

"It's one route we'll go."

"Started your neighborhood sweep yet?"

"The team's forming up now."

I walked over to a window and pointed out my friend to Charlie.

"Make sure someone talks to that old guy there. The one with the suspenders."

"What's special about him?"

"He lives next door. I talked to him when I was here, looking for Gomez. The guy doesn't work, he's home all day and his hobby's checking out anything on the block that moves. He might have seen something."

Some thoughts were beginning to form in my mind. Some loose ideas that I wanted to discuss with Charlie.

"Any chance of our getting together tomorrow?" I asked. "Got some ideas we could chew over."

Charlie grinned.

"Just like the old days, huh Will? Like we used to do."

The way Charlie and I worked, when we were partners in Homicide, every once in a while we'd get out of the stationhouse and go someplace where we could talk, uninterrupted. We'd put ideas about the case out on the table – we called them "killing scenarios". See if anything made sense.

I know some of those relationship guru types would call what we were doing, "free association," But "killing scenarios" worked for us

"Just like the old days," I agreed.

So, the next afternoon, with Lu still out of town, Charlie and I met at our apartment. By that time, Charlie was able to fill me in on some of the details about Gomez' killing.

"The coroner places time of death around six or seven pm," Charlie said. "We got the call at 8:30, a black and white got there fifteen minutes later, the uniforms discovered the body and they called it in."

"Who called the police?"

"It was your friend, the old coot in the suspenders. You were right about him. If it moves on the block, he knows about it. And in this case, if it doesn't move, he knows about that, too."

"Meaning?"

"The reason the guy called it in, was because he didn't see Carlos go out and pull his car into the driveway. Seems Gomez had one habit the old man got to know. Carlos would come home, park on the street, then if he was in for the night, by no later than eight o'clock, he'd pop out and pull his car into the driveway."

"And Carlos didn't do it last night? And the old guy noticed that, and figured something was wrong?"

"You got it."

"Gee, Charlie, maybe LAPD should hire him to do stakeouts,"

"Be better than some of the donut dunkers we got doing them now," Charlie agreed.

"What was the weapon?" I asked.

"Not a 9 millimeter, like was used to kill George Clemson."

"Well, that sort of blows some of the air out of my first scenario," I said.

"You mean, that the same person killed both George and Carlos?" Charlie asked.

"Well, yeah. It would have been neat if the same model weapon had been used for both killings. We'd have a definite tie-in, then. But still, I bet it wouldn't be the first time the same killer used two different weapons to kill two different victims."

"You're probably right," Charlie agreed.

There was a short pause in the conversation, and then Charlie asked, "Okay, Will, got any more killing scenarios for us to hash over?"

"As a matter of fact, yes. Did you ask Joan Clemson where she was, when George was killed?"

"Whoa! That one's way, way out. You think she could have killed George? And written the letters?"

"Just a killing scenario notion, Charlie. And I'm not happy bringing it up. She's a nice lady. But she hates her father. And she's a very tough person. So I'm wondering about her possibly killing George out of spite for her father. Again, did you check out where she was, when George was killed?"

Charlie opened his case notebook and flipped through the pages until he found what he wanted.

"Joan Clemson was getting her hair done at that time. Had a six thirty appointment. Was there until 8 PM. Confirmed by her hairdresser and the salon owner."

I was relieved. I hadn't wanted to think about Joan as a possible killer, but I had to raise the possibility.

"Here's another killing scenario question," I said to Charlie. "What did Stanley Clemson tell you, about where he was, when George was killed?"

Charlie checked his notebook again.

"Stanley said he was at home, alone. Said he'd gone home earlier than usual, because he wasn't feeling well."

"Hey, we got something here," I told Charlie. "Stanley gave me a different story. Said he was at WorkOut, working with his personal trainer. I checked with WorkOut, and he was there, alright, but on Tuesday night, not Wednesday night."

"So he lied to both of us."

"Yup."

Charlie shook his head.

"We'll go back to him, of course, But Stanley as a killer? Knocking off his own brother? That's a hard one to believe, Will."

"Need I remind you of the Menendez Brothers, Erik and Lyle? Back in 1989? Nice looking, Beverly Hills young men, knocking off their own parents?"

Charlie nodded.

"You never know, do you?" said Charlie, ever the philosopher.

Chapter Twenty-Seven

"I'm hearing things about Clemson Automotive," Al Silverman told me, when he called my office late in the afternoon. I'd called Al after my scenario session with Charlie.

"Sorry to be getting back to you so late," Al explained, "but today is when we close tomorrow's issue."

"It's okay," I assured him. "What are you hearing?"

"My sources say Clemson is getting caught up on its older receivables. And that Carl Clemson has called off his discussions with Acme, to have Clemson Automotive acquired."

I thought about what Al had just told me.

"If he's catching up on his older receivables," I reasoned aloud, "then this means Clemson has gotten some new capital, right?"

"It would seem that way," Al agreed. "Probably got a new line of credit."

"But why drop the Acme acquisition?" I wondered.

Al laughed.

"You ought to know the answer to that, if you know Carl. The guy doesn't like to take orders from anyone. He probably only went into the Acme discussions because he was worried about his company's future. But now, with more cash, the future looks okay, so he dumps Acme."

Al paused, then asked, "Do you have anything for me yet, Will?"

"No. But like I promised, you'll get it when it's ready."

"I'm counting on it."

"You can," I assured him.

Rose poked her head in as I was hanging up the phone.

"Remember, you're meeting Joan Clemson at Adagio's for dinner at seven o'clock. Reservation's all made."

"Thanks."

"I'm leaving. You can manage on your own for the rest of the time you are in the office?" she asked, the Jewish Mother in her bursting forth.

"It'll be hard, but I think I'll be okay."

"Don't forget to turn the lights out," she said, getting in the last word. Some things never change.

I'd called Joan earlier in the day and asked if she could meet me for dinner. She didn't know about Carlos Gomez's killing yet. He rated only one paragraph in the Daily News and nothing in the L.A. Times. I knew she'd take it hard, so I wanted to be the one to tell her.

"There's something you want to say, isn't there, Will?" Joan asked, when we were having our coffee.

"It shows, huh?"

"Behind that tough guy exterior, you're just a big marshmallow, and I can see you're uncomfortable about something. What is it?"

"It's about Carlos Gomez, He's…he's dead."

Joan gasped.

"Dead? What happened?"

"He was shot. Last night. In his house."

Joan was silent, as she absorbed the news.

Then, "Do the police know who did it?"

"No."

"Do they have any ideas? Theories? Do they think it might be the same person who killed George?"

Joan was no dummy.

"You should have been a detective," I complimented her. "That's one of the things the police are checking out."

Joan sighed.

"I am so sorry. So…so… sorry. Even though he rejected me, I was going to keep trying to get through to him, I know I would have succeeded, eventually."

Her eyes were wet.

"I know I would have, Will."

"I'm sure you would have."

We were interrupted by the sound of my beeper. I took a quick look at the digital display. It showed Rose's home telephone number and the added numbers – 911.

This meant that Rose had to talk to me. Right then. It was important.

I explained this to Joan as I called Rose on my cell phone, which I'd brought with me, into the restaurant.

The modern private investigator and his electronic array!

"What's up?" I asked Rose, when she answered.

"Will! Lu has been shot!"

Chapter Twenty-Eight

"Lu's been shot!"

The words kept banging around in my head as I ran out of the restaurant, to drive to LAX, Los Angeles Airport. Lucky for me, there didn't seem to be any CHPS, California Highway Patrol Service, cars on either the 101 or the 405, because I probably broke every traffic rule in the book.

Rose had booked a seat for me on the 9:40 PM American Airlines flight to Cleveland. At the airport, I dropped my car in the parking garage and ran to American.

I got to the ticket counter about 15 minutes before boarding. Enough time for me to call Cleveland Clinic, the hospital where Rose told me Lu had been taken.

But hell, I might as well have not made the call, for all that I learned. Or to put it more accurately, didn't learn. The patient information desk couldn't tell me anything, except that Lu had been admitted, via the emergency room. I yelled a lot. I'm her husband, damn it! I need to know what's happening! But it didn't do any good. They had no more information.

It's a four-hour flight from Los Angeles to Cleveland. The plane was one of the older ones in the American fleet. No air to ground telephones for passenger use. No way for me to call the hospital again.

The four hours felt like four years, as I sat there, worrying what I'd find when I got to the hospital. I had spoken with Rose again, from LAX before boarding. But all she could tell me was that she answered a call from a Cleveland policeman, who told her Lu was shot and was in surgery. He said he'd call back with more details when he had them, but he hadn't called by the time I boarded.

What I couldn't stop thinking about was, the goddamn Mob! The Cleveland bent noses!

Was this a mob hit on Lu? As revenge against me?

When Lu first told me she was going to Ohio, and the trip would include Cleveland, I did some worrying about it. Because three years ago, on another investigation I was doing, I found information that I turned over to the LAPD, and three members of the Family had gone to prison.

But this wasn't the way the Mob usually operated. No hits on women. Especially the wives. Some kind of a code of honor.

But the code had been broken! And Lu was shot. And all I could think about was, how and where in Cleveland, to get a piece and to go after them. Every damn one of them!

Stupid, Will! Stupid! That's not going to get you anywhere. You have to concentrate on Lu. Lu, on that operating table.

Oh, God! I'm scared I'll lose her.

That's not going to happen. It can't and it won't.

This is what I got to keep telling myself.

We landed at Hopkins International Airport at 4:40 am, Cleveland time. I ran out of the airplane and into the terminal, worrying about getting a cab at this hour.

"Jonas? Will Jonas?"

I stopped and looked at the man calling me. He put out his hand.

"Sergeant Harry Kalinsky, Cleveland PD. I'm here to get you to the hospital. Charlie Black called me."

"What about Lu? What can you tell me about my wife?"

Kalinsky shook his head.

"Only that she's still being operated on. Come on. I've got a car waiting outside."

A Cleveland Police Department black and white was parked curbside, engine running.

"Lights on. Siren all the way, Bill," Kalinsky told the driver, as he and I got into the back.

"I really appreciate this," I told Kalinsky.

"It's the least we can do," he said. "We're here for you. One cop to another. Want you to know that."

Once Kalinsky and I were in our seats, the driver took off, and twenty-five minutes later, we were at the hospital, where Kalinsky led me to the third floor, to a waiting room in the operating wing. Two men were in the room, and the older of them, he looked like he was in his mid-fifties, made the introductions.

"Mr. Jonas, I'm Captain Clarence Snyder, Cleveland PD. And this is Detective Sergeant Caleb Smith. He's leading the investigation into your wife's shooting."

"Call me Will," I said. "Please, what can you tell me about Lu?"

"We have word from the operating room that they're finishing up, and the doctor will be out soon, to talk to us," Snyder said. "Other than that, we have nothing new to tell you right now."

I turned to Detective Smith.

"Do you know what happened?"

"As near as we can piece it together, your wife had left her car and was walking to her room, when she was shot. She was hit twice. Both in the chest. No one heard the shots, but your wife managed to crawl to the next room and to knock on the door. Fortunately, someone was in that room, and called 911."

"No idea who did it?"

"Not yet. Except, I did talk to your former partner, and he filled me in, on your encounter with the Cleveland mob, three years ago. I've got a team following up on that angle right now."

We all turned as a man dressed in operating room greens came through the swinging doors, from the operating wing.

Snyder made the introductions.

"Dr. Gelman, this is Will Jonas, the husband."

"How is Lu?" I demanded.

Gelman clearly was happy to smile at my question, as he answered it.

"Long term, she'll be alright. For a while, it was close. She lost a lot of blood. Fortunately, neither bullet hit anything vital. Recovery will take time and plenty of rehab, but she is going to be fine."

"Can I see her?"

"Not for at least a couple of hours. She is in Recovery. Totally out. Pumped full of Kliozonat, to ease the pain. We'll let you see her, as soon as possible."

After Gelman went back inside, Snyder and Smith left. They both gave me their home telephone numbers and made me promise to call them if I needed anything. Once a cop, always a cop. That's how they were treating me. Even if I am retired.

Kalinsky said he wanted to stay on for a while we got some coffee out of the vending machine and sat down in the waiting room.

"That's quite a lady you have there," Kalinsky told me. "Tough. Not many people could've dragged themselves over to that next room, a good forty feet away, after taking two in the chest."

I shook my head, regretfully.

"When Lu told me she was going to Ohio, probably including Cleveland, I was worried. Because of what I had done to three of the Cleveland Mob guys in Los Angeles, three years ago. Got them sent to prison.

"But I told myself, they don't hit wives. Against their code of honor, if you can call it that. Yeah, unusual for the Mob to do so."

"Only, not as unusual as it used to be," Kalinsky answered. "Things are getting different nowadays. You were a cop in Los Angeles, right? Well, didn't things change over the years? What you could count on at one time – got very different at a later time, right?"

"Yeah, you're right. I know what you mean."

We sat silently, then. Kalinsky staying on because I'd once been a cop, and he was one, and there was that special bond among people who were on the job. Cops don't leave other cops alone in a hospital waiting room. It's as simple as that.

After a while, I don't know how long, Kalinsky's beeper went off and he walked out to the hall to take the call. He came back a few minutes later, a smile on his face.

"We got the guy who shot your wife."

I was surprised. Mob guys don't get caught that easily. Especially hit men.

Kalinsky reported, "Seems your wife was the victim of a druggie mugger. The hophead was out, trying to get some cash for his next fix. Well, after he shot Lu, he went to another motel nearby, and tried to mug a woman who'd just parked her car.

"Unlucky for him, the woman is a martial arts instructor, in town for a convention. She's got a black belt, they tell me. Anyway, she subdued the guy, called 911 and held him down until the police arrived."

"And the connection to Lu?" I asked.

"When the uniforms searched him, they found a 22 caliber weapon, two shells fired. The gun still smelled. The arresting officers had heard the all points on your wife, they put it together, confronted the guy and he confessed. Said he never meant to use the gun, but Lu started to fight back when he grabbed her, he panicked, and shot her."

"I'll be damned," I said, "and all along I thought it was a Mob hit."

"We were thinking that, too," Kalinsky agreed. "Goes to show you, doesn't it? It's all a matter of how you look at something, Will. The angle you're looking from. The perspective."

"You get no argument from me," I agreed.

"Mr. Jonas?"

A nurse had come into the waiting room.

"Are one of you gentlemen Mr. Jonas?" she asked.

"That's me."

"Mrs. Jonas is awake, now. She wants to see you."

Chapter Twenty-Nine

I don't like hospitals.

It isn't that I've got a phobia or anything, but, and don't laugh, I start to feel all kinds of aches and pains when I'm in one. This hurts, that feels like it isn't right, maybe I have cancer. Or, maybe it's because I'm 57 years old, and something always seems to hurt?

This time around, though, I didn't have any of those feelings. The only thing on my mind was to see Lu. And to assure myself that she was going to be alright.

When I got to her bed in Recovery, Lu was lying very still. There were tubes in her everywhere. I thought she was asleep, but she must have felt me lean against the bed, because she opened her eyes.

"Will," she whispered, and then she drifted off.

I took her hand in mine and squeezed a little. She returned the squeeze and opened her eyes again,

"Not...supposed...to happen," she whispered. "Stupid. I...was stupid. To fight back."

"But you're going to be fine," I assured her. "The doctor said you'll be fine.

"And another thing," I continued, "they caught the guy. The guy who shot you."

"Good..."

I bent and kissed Lu on the forehead. Sure, I would have preferred the lips, but the oxygen line going into her nose kind of made that hard to do.

"That feels good," she said, and she drifted off again.

The nurse who'd brought me into the room, came back.

"You have to leave now, Mr. Jonas. Your wife needs to rest."

I didn't want to leave, but the nurse was right, of course. I bent down and kissed Lu's forehead again. From somewhere in her sleep, she must have felt my kiss, because she smiled just a bit.

I was in Cleveland for three days. Each day, Lu got better, a little stronger. The fortunate thing about the shooting, was that the weapon used was small caliber, a .22. Yes, it can kill, if the bullets hit the right parts of the body. But if they don't, then death is less likely. With Lu, the seriousness of her condition was due more to her loss of blood and to the general trauma brought on by the shooting.

The day after I got to Cleveland, Lu's sister arrived from Chicago. Janine was a ten-year-older version of Lu. She and I got along fine, the couple of times she came to Los Angeles, to visit.

As Lu improved, my mind went back to thinking about the case in Los Angeles. A lot of new ideas, scenarios, wandering around in my head. I tried to keep that part of my brain out of Lu's hospital room, but she knew me too well. She could see that I was giving the case a lot of thought, and that I had things I wanted to do.

"It's that obvious?" I asked, embarrassed, when Lou confronted me.

She laughed, and that was a good sound to hear. This was the third day after the shooting, and Lu was sitting in a chair, propped up with pillows and a foot rest.

"That brain of yours is just itching to get back to Los Angeles and finish off the Clemson case," Lu said. "I can see it all over your face."

"I...I'm sorry..."

"Don't be, you idiot. You're just acting like you always act, and that's how, and why, I love you."

This time, there weren't any tubes in the way, so I gave Lu a big one, right on the lips. It felt good.

"Never did it on a hospital bed," I leered, kidding.

"Not going to, either," Lu laughed, not kidding.

She motioned for me to sit down on the bed, next to her chair. She took my hand in both of hers and looked at me.

"I love you, Will. You know what worried me more than anything else, when I was bleeding all over that parking lot? That I was going to die and never see you again. And it wasn't the dying that was so awful. It was the thought of not seeing you. Does that make any sense to you?"

"Makes perfect sense to me. It's the same way I'd feel."

Lu put her hand out and touched my cheek.

"You need to go back to Los Angeles, Will."

"No..." I started to protest.

"Yes, Lu countered. "Look, I love having you here, with me. But Janine will be here until I'm discharged, probably in a few days, the doctors are telling me. And then, I'm going back to Chicago with her, to stay at her house for a week or two. Then I'll be back in Los Angeles."

"You...sure you won't mind?" I asked, feeling guilty as hell.

Lu held her hands up, palms down, as if delivering a blessing.

"I give you dispensation," she intoned. "Get Thee back to the City of Angels and solveth that damned case."

"Priests don't swear," I pointed out.

"Irish priests sometimes do," Lu corrected me, "but only when they're telling some stubborn guy what he needs to do."

Chapter Thirty

Yeah, I did want to get back to Los Angeles. I'd been doing a lot of thinking the last couple of days. Sitting at Lu's bedside, I'd had plenty of time to do so while she was resting, sleeping.

And one of the things that kept going through my head was something Harry Kalinsky said, when he found out that Lu's assailant had been a druggie, not a Mob assassin.

"It's all a matter of how you look at something, Will. The angle you're looking from. The perspective."

His words were making me rethink some things about the Clemson case.

I made two calls to Los Angeles the day before I left Cleveland.

The first was to Al Silverman. I asked him to check out two questions I had about Clemson Automotive. And I promised him again that he'd have an exclusive story when the case was over.

The second was to Charlie Black. Before I got into my side of the conversation, Charlie had some news for me.

"Schlesinger is in the clear. His alibi, about playing cards the night George Clemson was killed, does check out. And boy, is he pissed at you for thinking he might be the killer."

"I'll live with it", I said. "What about Carlos Gomez?"

"We haven't nailed anyone yet, but we're hearing on the street that it may be a low level drug deal gone bad. Makes sense, since we've also heard that Carlos was dealing. Given the circumstances, we may never find anyone to hang the killing on. No big loss, though. We get a half dozen like it every week."

After he finished, I told Charlie what I wanted him to do.

"The first part," he said, "that I can find out pretty easily. But the other part, that's something else."

He thought for a moment before continuing.

"I'll need to call in a few favors for that one. There's a detective sergeant who owes me. Good guy. He'll know how to get the information, if anyone can."

"When I get back, let's get together."

"Another scenario session?"

"Yes."

"Want to give me a hint?"

"Not until we meet, and you have the information. It'll make more sense then, I hope."

"Okay, keep your old partner in suspense. See if I care. And by the way, Carl Clemson is complaining about you again. To everyone. How come you're still working on this case, because he fired you! How come you talked to Schlesinger? Now, he wants your license pulled."

"How'd he find out I was still on the case?"

"Our pain-in-the-ass Manny Soto."

"Well, I guess Carl doesn't like old memories stirred up. Past partners like Schlesinger. Their breakup wasn't a happy one."

"The point, Will, is this. Clemson is going for your license. You'll get the heat when you get back."

"I can hardly wait."

"Yeah, I thought you'd be overwhelmed with fear."

"Got any more good news for me?"

"Well, the weather's great. Going to be real nice tomorrow."

"Hey, Charlie, that's nothing new. Tomorrow is always nice in Southern California."

Chapter Thirty-One

I landed at LAX late the next morning and went straight to my office, where Rose brought me up to date on what was happening with my other clients.

One of the good things about Rose is that her Jewish Mother ways not only work on me, they work on my clients, too. Dropping just the right amount of Jewish Guilt, Rose had informed each client about Lu's shooting, which she called "her brush with death." Yes, she did say that!

"So we need to be patient until Will can leave her bedside and come back and take care of your business, won't we?" she told me she had said to each client.

Now, I ask you, how could any client be shabby enough to want work done on his account, when I was at my wife's bedside as she suffered through her brush with death?

Thank you, Rose.

There were a bunch of messages waiting for me. Most of them I put aside, to answer later. There was one, though, that I wanted to return right away. It was from Al Silverman.

"Welcome back, Will," Al said. "I hope your return means your wife is on the mend?"

"She is, and thanks for asking."

"I'm sure you want to know what I found out?"

"Yes, please."

"On that first question you asked me to check, you understand I had to be real careful, asking around, about something like that. It's not the kind of question you blabber about. Anyway, I checked a number of reliable sources, and no one has heard anything about Carl Clemson being sick, being in poor health."

"You're sure?"

"As sure as my sources can be. If Clemson has a health problem, it's a well-kept secret. No one has heard anything."

"Okay, Al."

I wasn't surprised. If my scenario was right, then this was the answer I was expecting.

"But on the second question you asked me to check out," Al continued, "I had better luck. Yes, there are rumors that Clemson is shopping his company again, this time to General Parts. They're even bigger than Acme."

This was good news, too. It fit right in to what I was thinking.

"Al, I'll be back in touch," I promised him.

In that pile of messages, there was one from Manny Soto, telling me to call him as soon as I got back to Los Angeles. I knew what that conversation would be about, so I threw the message slip in the round file.

My next call was to Joan Clemson.

"Will, it's good to hear from you. How is Lu?"

"Recovering. Doing fine, thank you."

"I felt so awful for you, when you got that call. It must have been horrible, flying to Cleveland."

"It was. But it's all turning out okay. Lu will be fine, her doctor says."

"I'm so glad."

"Joan, we need to talk. About...the case. George's killing."

"You've got new information?" she asked eagerly.

"Maybe. Maybe not. But I have to talk to you. Can we get together?"

"Of course. When?"

"I'm not certain. I need to check out a few things, first. Probably tomorrow. I'll call you when I know for sure."

"That will be fine."

I hung up and began to feel lousy.

Did I have new information, Joan had asked me.

Yes, Joan, I have new information. Only it's not very flattering for your father. I know you say you hate him, but he's still your father.

I took a deep breath, trying to ease the tension in my neck. Talking to Joan wasn't going to be easy, but it had to be done.

My next call was to Charlie Black.

"Soto was just here, asking if you'd contacted me," Charlie said. "You're calling from Cleveland, right?" he joked.

"Actually, Columbus. We got grounded. Engine trouble. I may not get back for weeks, you can tell him."

"No thanks," he said, and then added, "I've got some interesting answers to the questions you asked me to check out. But I can't talk about them from here."

"So, let's get together, tonight."

We decided to meet at Charlie's house. I'd been there many times, especially in the first months after my wife, Vera, died, and Charlie's wife, Sheila, had made it a point of having me over for dinner. Charlie was both my partner and a good friend. And Sheila and Vera had also been close friends.

Charlie and Sheila lived in Simi Valley, a bedroom community just north and west of Los Angeles County. It's a city that has grown a lot in the last 20 years, and it's also home to a very large number of LAPD cops and L.A. County Sheriffs deputies.

Such a large number, in fact, that Simi is considered one of the safest communities in the Los Angeles areas.

Or to put it another way, in Simi, if you decide to stick up a 7-11, chances are, at least one or two of the customers in the store will be off-duty, but still-armed, cops. And who'd want to try and pull a robbery, given those odds?

After one of Sheila's usual great dinners, Charlie and I went into his den at the back of the house, and Charlie started our meeting.

"The first thing you asked me to look into, you were right. So tell me, how'd you know about that key man insurance?"

"From what Al Silverman told me. He said that all of a sudden, Clemson Automotive was out of its cash flow trouble. It was getting caught up on its older receivables. And Clemson also had cancelled his discussions for Acme to acquire Clemson.

"Al figured Clemson Automotive must have gotten a new line of credit from one of its banks, and I went along with that reasoning.

"But while I was in Cleveland, I began to wonder about that. I asked myself, if Clemson Automotive was having financial problems, then why would a bank lend it more money?

"Didn't make any sense to me, so I started thinking about other ways that Clemson Automotive could have come into some new capital.

"It couldn't be from Acme, because Carl had walked away from that potential deal.

"And I didn't think it was from a private investor. That wouldn't be Carl's style, to let some private party in on the action, and risk losing control of his company.

"So, what was left, I asked myself.

"And then I remembered the Corrington case we worked on, maybe ten years ago. You remember that one?"

Charlie thought for a few seconds.

"That was where this guy Corrington, the president of the company, was killed in a car crash, leaving his wife with lots of debts, because they were living way beyond their means.

"And it turned out his company got fifteen million dollars from the insurance company, because of a key man policy they were carrying on him. And we convinced the chairman of the board to give five million of it to the widow."

Charlie laughed.

"Of course, it wasn't too hard to convince the guy, after we followed up on the rumors we heard, about his liking prostitutes, and we took those pictures of him, with one of those ladies of the night. And threatened to give the shots to his wife."

Charlie laughed again at the memory, and then continued.

"And so, to answer what you asked me about, I found out that Clemson Automotive has key man insurance on all three of the Clemsons'...Carl, George and Stanley. Ten million on each of them."

I picked up our discussion.

"Ten million, Charlie. Ten million cash. And that's how Clemson got caught on his older receivables. And why he cancelled his discussions with Acme. Because he got the cash he needed...from the key man insurance payout on George's death."

I paused, to let Charlie think about what I'd just said, and then I continued.

"You know that I always questioned robbery as the motive for George's killing. A robber who panicked and ending up killing George? Remember how I told Soto that was a weak scenario?"

"I remember," Charlie answered.

"Well, Charlie, I think...Carl...killed...George. He killed him for the ten million dollar key man insurance payoff. The money he needed, to save his beloved company."

"Whoa," Charlie objected, "that's one helluva jump. I mean, this is a big time, well known businessman. And he kills his son for the insurance money?"

"Okay, I see your point," I conceded. But for now, just go

along with me on this?"

Charlie nodded, and I continued.

"What about the other thing I asked you to find out?"

Charlie went to his note pad.

"You got a great memory," he said. "You remembered everything on that prescription label, just right. The label on that pill bottle you picked up off the floor, in Carl's office. How come you thought about it now?"

"Because of something the surgeon said about Lu, when he came out of the operating room. It didn't hit me, when he first said it. I only thought about it, later, when I was taking a fresh look at the whole case. Doing what that Cleveland cop told me did on his cases. Look at things from a new perspective.

"And then it came to me. The surgeon mentioned a drug, Kliozonat. Said he'd given it to Lu, as a heavy duty pain killer. But when I gave that bottle back to Carl Clemson, after I found it under his desk, he said he was taking the pills for, to quote his words, 'damned allergies.' You don't use heavy-duty pain killers for allergies. And so I got curious about it."

I nodded toward Charlie, and asked him, "So, what did you find out?

"My contact in the New York Police Department had an easy enough time getting Dr. Ghajar's address from the pharmacy. He had a tougher time getting any information from Dr. Ghajar. All that doctor-patient confidentiality stuff. But Ghajar finally gave in. Covered his ass, of course. Told my guy the reason he was giving in, and that's interesting in itself."

"What do you mean?"

"Well, it seems Clemson went to Ghajar out of the blue. Wasn't referred to him, or anything like that. And Clemson told Ghajar a strange story. He said he'd been living in Europe for many years, and had just gotten back to this country. Also, he said he didn't have any medical insurance, and he paid his bill in cash, before he left.

"Even stranger, he told Dr. Ghajar there was no doctor to refer the records to. And he said he wanted to take all the records and x-rays with him. He said he was going back to Europe.

"And here's the final strange thing. Clemson gave as his address and New York residence, a hotel in Manhattan, where, when my guy checked, they had no record of any Carl Clemson ever staying there."

"What does that sound like to you, Charlie?" I challenged him.

"Clemson didn't want anyone to know anything about his visit to Dr. Ghajar."

I asked, "What was Clemson hiding? Did your guy find out why Clemson went to Ghajar?"

"Cancer," Charlie told me. "Ghajar diagnosed Clemson with prostate cancer. Too advanced for any effective treatment, though. It's terminal. Clemson's got maybe two years, at the outside.

"And here's the craziest thing of all. Clemson refused any treatment from Ghajar. They got things they can do. Even if they can't stop the disease, they can make it a little more bearable. But Clemson said no go all of that.

"The only thing Clemson asked for, was something for the pain that Ghajar told him was coming, when the cancer reaches its late stages. Ghajar wasn't wild about giving him the Kliozonat prescription, but under the odd circumstances, he decided he might as well."

We were both silent as we thought about what we'd learned. I finally spoke.

"Here's what I figure. Clemson learns he has cancer, and that he's terminal. He has maybe two years at the outside. His company, the most important thing in his life, we know that, his company is in trouble. It needs money. Clemson knows about the key man insurance, of course, and like I said before, he decides to kill George, to get the money he needs."

"And like I said before," Charlie comes back at me, "that is one helluva jump. To kill his own son for the insurance money?"

"Except...George wasn't Carl's son!"

Charlie looked at me, puzzled.

"George wasn't Carl's son?"

"Yup. Not genetically."

I told Charlie what Bill Schlesinger had told me, about the affair Emily Clemson had with the pharmacist, Richard Bellows. How Emily got pregnant, how Bellows left town, and how Carl had taken on the fatherhood because of the difficulties he and Emily were having at the time, in conceiving.

"But he brought the kid up," Charlie pointed out. "Raised him as his own. You don't think that meant anything to Clemson?"

"No, I don't," I countered. "He probably hated the kid from the start. George was a constant reminder of Emily's having been unfaithful to him. To him! Not something someone like Carl could accept. That his wife, even if only once, had preferred another man over him. Look how he brought George up. He beat on him every day. Made him an emotional cripple. You ask me, I don't think Carl had any love, any good feelings for George. He loved his damned company a lot more. And yes, I do believe he'd kill George, if it was a way he could save his company."

"But what about the letters?" Charlie asked. "What about those? And the phone call?"

I answered, "I think Carl did all of that himself. Remember, I said from the beginning, that there was something odd about those letters? They threatened, but they never demanded anything. Never asked for a payoff.

"And now, I think I know why. Because if there had been a demand for a payoff, then that would have meant a time and place for the dropoff of the money. And how could there be a dropoff, if Clemson was writing the letters to himself? He certainly couldn't take the chance of going to pick up the money.

"I say, the letters were fake. Clemson sent them to himself, then he told the police about them. And he also called himself on the phone and left that message on his voice mail. Remember, the voice was so disguised, there was no chance of identifying the caller, not even as to sex."

"So he sets up the threat," Charlie picks up on my line of reasoning, "and he gets the police into it, and then, at night, when he knows George is working late, he kills him. Makes it look like a robbery gone bad."

"And," I point out, "it makes it look like the threatening letters and the phone call are real. No matter that it's George who's killed. That's a close enough tie to Carl, to make those threats look legitimate.

"And to top it off, Charlie, he collects on the insurance, and presto, Clemson Automotive is back in good shape."

"Hold on a minute, though, Will. Maybe Clemson Automotive is in good shape, but Carl isn't. He's gonna die within a year or two. What about that?"

"What about it?" I threw back at Charlie. "You have to remember that the two most important things in Carl Clemson's life are Clemson Automotive, and, how people see Carl Clemson as a successful entrepreneur, a big time, hot shot businessman. The guy's an egomaniac. That's clear enough. His public image is very important to him.

'Now, with his company back in good shape, thanks to the key man insurance money, Carl can go to any company he wants. There are others besides Acme. And he can work a much better acquisition deal. One he can be proud of. And in fact, according to Al Silverman, Clemson's already doing that. He's talking to a bigger company, called General Parts."

"No one knows he has cancer," Charlie picks up on my line of thought, "so he goes strong, into his discussions with General. His company is solid, maybe he signs a long term employment contract…"

"And after all that's done," I pick it up again, "then what do you know? Carl goes to his regular doctor for a routine checkup, and damn! They discover he has prostate cancer. Advanced. Terminal. Well, too bad, General Parts. You'll just have to do without me. But I sure am leaving you with a solid company, right?"

"And out he goes," Charlie finishes up, "the business leader who built a fine company, then sold it off on good terms, and isn't it terrible, though, how he is dying? Candles and violins in the background."

We were both quiet for a while. Then Charlie broke the silence.

"This is one fine scenario we just built, Will. But you know, and I know, it's all circumstantial. We have nothing to back up anything we're saying. There is no way the Department can move against someone of Clemson's stature, based on what we've reasoned out here. From Soto, right up to the Chief, they're not going to buy it."

"I know that," I agreed.

"So, what do we do, now?" Charlie asked.

"I talk to Joan Clemson."

Chapter Thirty-Two

Do you remember Louis The Fisherman, my super snitch? Let me refresh your memory.

Back when I was starting on the Clemson case, I met with Louis, told him about the investigation, and asked him to poke around and see if he could learn anything about who might be writing those threatening letters to Carl Clemson.

I hadn't heard anything from The Fisherman since the night we met, so I figured that he hadn't been able to dig up anything of use to me.

But when I got to my office the next morning, Rose handed me a telephone message slip. No name on it. Just three different cell phone numbers.

Had to be Louis, I figured. He liked to say that a moving target was harder to hit, and who could argue the point, since he's still alive.

The first number was busy, so I dialed the second.

"Yes," was the way Louis always answered.

"It's Will Jonas. You called me?"

"I most certainly did. Got some good information for you. Ought to use up the whole five hundred you started me out with."

"Let's hear it, and then we'll decide," I said, knowing I was only mouthing meaningless words. Louis had already decided.

"Guy I know down in South Bay sold a gun to Clemson," Louis said.

Right there, I agreed with Louis. This information was worth the whole five hundred.

"How'd you come up with that?" I asked. "What I mean is, how did your guy know it was Clemson?"

"I was asking around for information, and when I talked to this dude, he remembered seeing his picture in the Times, after the killing. And he told me he sold the guy the gun."

"What kind of gun?" I asked, hoping I'd get the right answer.

"He says it was a 9 millimeter. That what you're looking for?"

"Amen, Louis. That's exactly what I was looking for."

To me, this took the case from "circumstantial" to "real."

We already had motive – the insurance money. And now we had a gun, right caliber and all.

"Can I get your guy to testify to that sale?" I asked, already knowing the answer.

Louis laughed, and that was answer enough, but he also spelled it out for me.

"You goin' soft in the head, Will? You know my business. I sell information. I don't supply a live person, so the heat can charge the guy with illegally selling a weapon,"

"Well, no harm in asking..."

"And no harm in being asked," Louis assured me.

"Good work, Louis. And you're right. It's worth the whole five hundred."

"You want me to keep poking around, Will?"

"Sure."

You never know with Louis. Letting him poke some more might turn up something else. Worth the money, I figured.

After Louis and I were through, I called Charlie. I was sure this was information he could use, to push the point with Soto and his superiors, that Carl Clemson should be questioned.

Charlie wasn't in, but I didn't want to leave my name. I was concerned that Manny Soto might spot any telephone slip, asking Charlie to call me back, and I didn't want to get Charlie into trouble. I figured I'd catch up with him later in the day.

Rose buzzed and I picked up.

"There is a Mr. Walter Wilson out here," she told me. "He wants to see you."

"I don't know any Walter Wilson, and I don't have an appointment with him. Who is he, and what does he want?"

"He says he is with the Department of Consumer Affairs."

Now I knew what it was about, and thanks to a discussion I'd had with Jack Goodman, the lawyer who originally recommended me to Carl Clemson, I was ready for Walter Wilson.

"Send him in," I told Rose, "and don't offer him any coffee. He's not going to be here long enough to drink it."

Rose brought Wilson in, and instead of being pissed at him, I felt sorry for the guy. Judging by how he carried himself, sort of hunched over, Wilson wasn't in my office because he wanted to be here. He'd been sent by someone in the Department, I was sure, because of pressure from Clemson. And it had to do with my private investigator license, of course, because that piece of paper was issued and supervised by the California State Department of Consumer Affairs.

"Let me make this easy for you, Mr. Wilson," I said, getting up from my desk, walking across my office and opening the door Rose had just shut. "Okay, you've delivered your message about the Department being in charge of my PI license. And you've told me a complaint has been made against me, by Carl Clemson.

"But I know the rules, and if this was a legitimate complaint, rather than just some pressure being applied by Clemson, then there'd be a case worker assigned, an investigation, a hearing, and a letter outlining the complaint and the case procedure.

"There's been none of that, so I know the only reason you're here is because your boss said to go on down and scare me off the Clemson case, because Carl knows the governor, or the Department head, or dozen other heavyweight characters.

"Okay, Mr. Wilson, You can go back and tell them I'm scared. Really scared. You can even tell them I pissed in my pants. All over my floor. Hell, you can tell them whatever you want. I don't care.

"But what I do care about, is that you get out of my office right now. You understand? Right now."

For emphasis, I walked over and stood next to Wilson. Six four over maybe five eight? Wilson knew what to do. He left,

"Such a shtarka," Rose kidded me.

"A...shtarka? What's that mean?"

"It means, a big one. Like you. That little man never had a chance,"

Then Rose turned anxious.

"Will, are you in trouble with this license megilah?"

"No way," I assured her. "I've discussed it with Jack. He'll represent me, if there's ever a hearing. But that's something that would be way in the future. And it's not to worry about."

What there was to worry about, however, was my meeting with Joan Clemson. It was set for mid-afternoon, at her apartment.

I'd told Joan we had to meet someplace quiet, that I had a lot to go over with her, and with no interruptions. She'd suggested her condo and that was fine with me.

We met there at 3:00.

"This isn't going to be an easy conversation, Joan," I said, as we sat down in her living room, "and I want to apologize for that, before we start."

Joan smiled at me.

"Please, Will. I know you have only my best interests at heart, so there's no need to apologize. Whatever you have to tell me... just tell me."

I took a deep breath.

"Okay, here it is. I believe your father...killed George."

Joan gasped, and for a second, I thought she was going to faint. But then, she took several deep breaths.

"I...you...how can you say something like that? How can this be?"

"I'm so sorry about this, Joan, and I'm only telling you now, because I'm quite certain about it. And the way things are going, I think it is inevitable that your father will be brought in for questioning. Of course," I cautioned, "he doesn't know anything about this."

Joan bit her lip. She clasped and unclasped her hands.

"Will, what are you talking about? Please tell me!"

I gave Joan the details. Pretty much a replay of the scenario Charlie and I had put together last night at his house.

When I was finished, Joan didn't talk for a minute or two, and I also kept quiet.

She finally spoke.

"It does look pretty definitive, doesn't it?"

"I think so. Of course, I could be wrong. I could be."

"But you don't think so."

"Joan, I did this kind of work for 30 years. As a homicide detective with LAPD. And when things feel right to me...well...they usually are."

She was silent again, and as I watched her face, I saw her go from shock, to concern, to anger.

"That horrible, horrible man! To kill his own son! For what? For insurance money to save his beloved company?

Joan held her hands up in front of her, as if strangling someone.

"If he were here right now, I could kill him myself!"

She began pacing around the room, shaking her head and pounding a fist into the palm of her other hand. She stood in front of the living room window, staring out, still shaking her head.

After a few minutes, she grew calmer and turned to me.

"What happens now, Will?"

I paused before answering. This was going to be the toughest part, because of what I now was going to ask Joan to do.

"Any good defense lawyer," I told her, "could make these facts that I've given you, go away and get lost. Too much of it is circumstantial, and the defense lawyer will argue that it leaves room for reasonable doubt. And remember, a jury is charged with reaching a "not guilty" verdict, if they feel there is reasonable doubt."

"But you don't feel there is reasonable doubt, do you?" Joan asked.

"No, I don't. But the defense lawyer will certainly push for it. And chances are, he'll get enough jurors convinced that he's right. And your father will walk away from this. Unless..."

"Unless what, Will?"

"Unless we have an eye witness to the killing. Someone who saw your father kill George."

Joan looked at me, her unspoken question clear on her face.

"And I believe there is such a person," I told her.

"Who?" she demanded.

"Stanley."

"No!"

Joan shook her head from side to side.

"How could you possibly believe that Stanley...that Stanley had anything to do with this? That he could be involved with killing George! They were close! Very close! Stanley simply isn't capable of something like this."

"Joan, I didn't say Stanley was involved. Hell, no!

"But I do think he saw it happen.

"And I'm also sure your father doesn't know Stanley saw him kill George.

"And I'm convinced the reason Stanley is acting so nervously, now, is because he doesn't know how to handle what's happened. He doesn't know what to do!"

"I...I don't understand what you mean," Joan said.

"I think Stanley's wrestling with a couple of problems," I explained. "And they're driving him nuts.

"First, he saw Carl kill George. Does he go to the police with that information? Does he turn his own father in? That's his first problem.

"But second, I think he's also very, very afraid."

"Of what?"

"He's afraid of your father. Stanley's afraid that...Carl might try and kill him, too!"

"My God! How could he think that?"

"Because he saw his father kill his brother, and be clever enough to get away with it.

"And because, by now, he's figured out why it happened. For the insurance money.

"And because Stanley has to know that there's also a ten million dollar policy on him. Does it take much more for Stanley, especially in his present, agitated frame of mind, to reach the conclusion that his own life might be in danger?"

"I can't believe any of what you're saying!" Joan shouted, jumping up and again pacing around the room.

I didn't do anything. Just sat there, I'd unloaded a lot on her, and I knew she had to work it out in her own mind, before we could go on to the next painful step that I wanted to talk to her about.

It took a few minutes, but Joan did finally sit down and talk to me.

"I...think...you're probably right. I...it's...so hard to understand any of this. But I'm afraid you're right. It does explain, doesn't it, why Stanley's been acting the way he has. If you're right, then it very much explains Stanley's agitated state."

"Where's Stanley now?" I asked. "Is he at the office?"

"No, He's away."

"Away?"

"He left yesterday. On a hiking vacation."

"Is that something he usually does?"

"As a matter of fact, yes. Only, he doesn't normally do it, at this time of the year.

"I asked him why he was going now, and he said he had to get away for a few days. Said he had a lot of things to think about. Now, I understand what he meant. God, my poor Stanley."

"When does he get back?"

"Tomorrow. Tomorrow afternoon."

"We have to talk to him, Joan. As soon as he gets back. We have to convince him that he must go to the police, and tell them what he saw."

"Of course," Joan agreed, dully, as she thought about the wreckage of her family.

"You'll call me tomorrow? When Stanley gets back? So we can see him, and talk to him?"

"Yes..."

Joan sat still, silent.

I reached over and took her hand.

"I know this is hell, Joan. I wish it could have been different. You don't know how much I wish that."

Joan looked at me and smiled weakly.

"I do know, Will."

"Can I do anything for you? Get you anything?"

Joan shook her head.

"No. I...I'd like to be alone, though. Got a lot to absorb. An awful lot. Could you leave now, Will? Please?"

I didn't want to go, but I did. It's what she wanted, and I felt that, right now, Joan knew what was best for her.

Chapter Thirty-Three

I went back to my office after the meeting with Joan, because I wanted to talk with Lu. It was her last night in the hospital, before going with Janine to Deerfield, a Chicago suburb.

I figured that if I went home, by the time I got there, it might be too late to call the hospital and get through to Lu's room, because Cleveland time was three hours later than Los Angeles.

"Hello, Will," Lu answered my call.

"How'd you know it was me?"

"Well, I've heard from everyone else who I expected to call, so I was sure it was you."

"Gee, you should have been a detective. You're good at detecting."

"No, thank you. One in the family is enough."

"You sound better."

"I am better, Will. Much better. Almost to the point where we could use the hospital bed the way you wanted to, when you were here. Remember?"

"Don't tempt me. I can still get the red eye out of LAX."

Lu laughed.

"It's good to hear that laugh," I told her. "I can't wait to hear it on a more regular basis. When are you coming back to Los Angeles?"

"Well, I told you about two weeks, but now, I think it might be more like ten days. It depends on how I feel, once I start trying to get around normally."

"Don't push too much, Lu, but make it as fast as you can."

"As fast as I can, Will. I love you. Good night."

"And I love you. Good night."

The phone rang, right after Lu and I had finished talking. It was Charlie.

"I just got home, and Sheila told me to call you."

"Right. I didn't want to leave a message at the stationhouse. Didn't want Soto to know I was contacting you."

"Thanks. He's been all over me today. Asking what I've got

137

new on the Clemson killing."

"You tell him anything about our scenario?"

"Nope. I still don't think I can, given how circumstantial it is, and that it involves such a heavyweight as Carl Clemson."

"Well, I think you'll be able to talk to him tomorrow, Charlie. I surely do."

"Whoa! How's that? What's up?"

"What's up, is that The Fisherman's come up with information that Clemson bought a gun from one of Louis's contacts. And, it's a nine millimeter. How's that grab you?"

"By the very shortest of hairs! That's good stuff, Will. So, Carl Clemson bought a weapon. Same caliber as the gun that was used to kill George Clemson. I'd say that's plenty to go to Soto with, and the Chief, and to make a move on Clemson. To bring him in for questioning."

As Charlie was talking, something he said set off an alarm bell in my head.

I'd said to Charlie that The Fisherman told me a contact of his had sold a nine millimeter to Clemson. In response, Charlie had said to me, "So, Carl Clemson bought a weapon..."

"Damn!" I interrupted Charlie.

"What?"

"Charlie, I think I may have just fucked up big time."

"What are you talking about?"

"Listen to me. You ready?"

"Yeah..."

I checked my notes before continuing.

"Okay. The Fisherman called me and said, and these are his exact words, 'One of my people down in the South Bay sold a gun to Clemson.' That's what he said. 'To Clemson.'

"I figured, without thinking, that he meant Carl Clemson. Why? Because the guy told The Fisherman he'd seen a picture in the Times, right after the murder.

"I have a pile of newspaper clippings on my desk, about the case, that Rose keeps adding to, every day. I'm looking at the clippings right now, and the big story about the murder has Carl's picture, not George's. But you know what? There's different editions of the Times. I get the San Fernando Valley edition. The Fisherman's contact probably gets the South Bay edition. Could have been a whole different story, and picture, there. And until I can find out what picture ran in the South Bay, I can't be sure which Clemson bought the gun."

"You didn't fuck up, Will," Charlie said. "You...almost...fucked up. Almost. Now, you gotta find out which Clemson, The Fisherman's guy meant."

"I'll try and reach The Fisherman right now. Call you back."

I hung up and pawed through the papers on my desk, looking for that telephone slip with The Fisherman's three cell phone numbers.

This time, I reached him on the first cell phone.

"Louis, I need to check something about what you told me," I said.

"And that is...?"

"You told me your contact sold a nine millimeter to Clemson. My question is, which Clemson? Carl? Or George?"

"Wait a minute while I check my notes."

Yes, that's right. He said he'd have to check his notes. Did I tell you from the start, that Louis was an entrepreneur of a snitch? A major league purveyor of information?

The man kept notes of his conversations! But not to worry about confidentiality. Louis once showed me some of his notes. They're in code. The words are English, but they don't make sense to anyone except The Fisherman. And that's Louis for you.

"Will?" Louis came back on the line. "It was George Clemson. That's who my guy sold the gun to."

"Shit!" was all I could manage.

"Sorry, Will. Facts are facts."

Philosophy wasn't something I needed right now.

I broke the connection.

Back to Charlie at home, who picked up on the first ring.

"And...?" he prompted.

"George Clemson bought the gun. Not Carl."

"George, huh? Okay...waiting for your callback, I started thinking about him buying the gun, and how that would play out."

"I've been thinking, too," I said. "Thinking that maybe George bought that gun to commit suicide. According to his wife, he was in a severe depression. Seeing a psychiatrist five times a week."

"Yeah, I see where you're heading. But George absolutely did not commit suicide."

"How do you know that?"

"Because he was shot three times," Charlie said, "and the coroner said the first shot was enough to kill him. Dead men don't commit suicide.

So the question is," Charlie continued, "how does this fit in with our idea that Carl killed George? And we also have to ask, how did Carl get a hold of the gun that George bought?"

We both thought for a time, and then I put out the first scenario.

"How about this?" I asked. "Carl and George are at Clemson Automotive, after hours. They get into an argument. Maybe about the General Parts acquisition. We know George was upset about Carl holding those talks without consulting him."

"They're arguing," Charlie continues the scenario, "in George's office. He's behind his desk. In anger, he pulls out the weapon. Carl, who's much bigger and stronger, wrestles it from George, and in his own fit of anger, he shoots George. Not once. But three times."

I contribute the next lines.

"Then, realizing what he's done, Carl tries to figure out how to get out of the mess. So, he takes George's wallet, to make it look like a robbery, hides it somewhere, along with the gun, and then he calls 911."

"By the time we get there," Charlie adds, "he's figured out his alibi. He told us, he heard the shots, he ran into George's office, and up to the desk, to see if he could help his son."

I pointed out, "That's how he explained his footprints being in the blood on the floor."

"Right," Charlie confirmed. "That's what he told us."

We both stopped talking, as we considered this new angle, this new scenario.

I was the first to speak.

"It works for me, Charlie. I liked it better when we thought Carl Clemson bought the gun. It was a cleaner scenario. But this one could be right."

"I agree." Charlie said. "Only now, since we can't tie Carl directly to the gun purchase, we're back to the circumstantial. And that means, again, that I can't go to Soto with it, and I can't bring

Clemson in for questioning. So, we still got our basic problem."

"I know," I said. "How do we nail Carl? Well, I think I have the answer."

"What's that?"

"Not 'what,' but 'who.' And the 'who' is Stanley Clemson."

Chapter Thirty-Four

Joan Clemson called the next afternoon, to tell me that Stanley was back. He was at home, she said, and we decided to go to him, there, unannounced.

When Stanley opened his front door and saw me, he stumbled backward.

"What is he doing here?" he shouted at Joan. "You didn't say he'd be with you!"

"We've got to talk, Stanley," Joan told him, forcefully, "and Will has to be part of it."

Stanley stared at us.

"Please, Stanley," Joan appealed to her brother.

Stanley stepped aside and let us in.

I had a good look at Stanley, as we sat down in his living room. The couple of days of hiking had given him some healthy looking outdoor color. But his eyes and mouth mirrored the stress he was under. Red-rimmed, his eyes darted in one direction or another. His mouth was set in a tight, thin line, except when his tongue came out to lick his dry lips.

Joan led the conversation, a tactic she and I had agreed upon.

"How was your hike?" she asked.

"Okay."

"Did you…have a chance to think about the things you wanted to think about?"

"What do you mean?"

"Before you left, you told me you had a lot to think about. So, I was wondering if you had done so."

Stanley didn't answer.

Joan continued.

"Stanley…" she said gently, "I know you're worried about what…happened to George. And I think it would be good, if you would talk to me, to us, about it."

"I don't know what you mean. I don't know what you're saying," Stanley said nervously.

Still continuing in a gentle tone, Joan said, "I know there are things bothering you about George's death. Things that I'm sure you'd feel better sharing with us. Please talk to us, Stanley."

"You don't know anything!" Stanley lashed out at Joan.

"You don't know what you're asking! You have no idea!"

"Yes, we have a very good idea," I broke into the conversation.

I waited until Stanley looked at me, and I had his attention.

"We know you saw your father kill George. You saw your father shoot your brother. And now, you don't know what to do."

"I wasn't there when George was killed! I told you that, already!"

"You lied," I cornered him. "You told me you were at Powertown. I checked. And I know you weren't there, when George was killed."

Stanley stared at me, increasingly nervous, but remaining silent.

"Please, Stanley," Joan pleaded. "I can see that you're being torn apart by whatever it is you know about George's killing. You can't go on this way. You must tell us. You must let us help you."

Stanley shook his head, slowly, softly. He looked at his sister, his face full of the pain he was feeling.

"Tell me something, Joan. How can I tell the police I saw my father, kill my brother? Do I now condemn my father, by telling the police he killed George? What good will that do? George is already dead. My father will be convicted, probably sentenced to die, if I tell the police what I saw. I hate him. But he is my father. Our father. Our mother's husband. How can I do this?"

Joan stood, walked to Stanley, and knelt in front of him. She took his hands in hers.

"It's awful, Stanley. Just awful what our father has done. He's not only killed George, he's also killed our entire family. He's driven me away. You know how badly he treats our mother. And, look how badly he's always treated you. You ask, how can you condemn your own father? I ask, is this man truly deserving of being your father? Our father? I think not. I feel not."

Joan put her arms around Stanley. He hesitated, and then he put his arms around her. They embraced, and they both began to weep quietly, softly.

Then, with his head buried in Joan's shoulder, Stanley started to talk in a muffled voice.

"I...saw him. Standing there. Holding the gun. And he shot George. Then he shot him again.

"And he shouted at George. He shouted, 'you can't do anything right. Even die right.'

"I watched him kill George, and shout those terrible words. And then I ran away. I couldn't stand seeing what was happening. I had to run away."

Stanley looked up at me, then.

"And I haven't known what to do!"

"What you need to do, is tell the police," I answered.

I stood and started walking toward the phone.

Joan stood and blocked my way.

No, Will," she said strongly. No!"

"What do you mean?"

"I mean, before we go to the police, Stanley and I, we have to see our father. We have to...ask him questions. We have to know...how could he do this to our family? I want him to explain that to us. To Stanley and me."

"It would be better if we went straight to the police, Joan. Let them do the confronting, the questioning."

Joan took hold of my shoulders and looked up at me, her eyes hard and cold. Damn! In this way, she was so much her father's daughter.

"You owe me, Will. I've done everything you've wanted, to help you on this investigation. You would not be here, today, if it wasn't for me. You owe me. You owe my family."

She was right. If Joan and Stanley wanted to confront their father, to demand that he explain to them how he could have done something so terrible as to kill George, then they had that right, as far as I was concerned.

"Okay," I said. "But I have to call Detective Black, to let him know what's happening."

"If he tries to stop us..." Joan began.

"He won't," I assured her. "He'll do what I ask."

"Fine."

I called Charlie, knowing he'd be in, because I'd called him earlier, alerting him to stand by, after I made the date to meet Joan at Stanley's.

I told him, then I turned to Joan and Stanley.

"Let's go."

Chapter Thirty-Five

Carl Clemson usually was in his office every evening until at least 7:30, Stanley told Joan and me, so that's where we went.

The building was closed, the front door locked. Stanley used his key to let us in through the double glass door entrance.

"Leave it unlocked," I told him.

Joan led the way, Stanley following, and then me, as we walked through the reception area, down the hall, and into Carl's office. He was seated at his desk, in shirtsleeves, reading a file.

Carl sensed our presence and looked up, surprised.

"What are you doing here?" he snapped at us.

"We're here to talk to you," Joan said, just as coldly, as she walked up to her father's desk.

Stanley followed her, reluctantly, while I hung back, sensing I should let this family affair play out on its own for now,

Carl ignored Joan and Stanley and glared at me

"And what the hell are you doing here? Get out of Clemson Automotive. I fired you."

"He's not working for you," Joan said. "And he stays."

Carl looked at Joan, then at Stanley, and then at me. No one said anything. He shrugged.

"Suit yourself. Now, what do you want?"

"The truth," Joan said.

"The truth? About what?"

"About George's death."

Carl leaned forward in his chair, his muscles tensing. Then he sat back, in control.

"I don't know what you mean. You want to know about George's death? Go to the police. They're running the investigation, not me."

Joan turned to Stanley.

"Tell him," she said, softly but firmly. "Tell him what you saw."

Stanley tried to stand straight, but he shriveled as his father glared at him.

"Stanley, tell him," Joan said repeated, this time in a harsher tone,

Then she took hold of Stanley's hand and spoke to him, again in a softer voice.

"You must, Stanley. For all of us."

Drawing strength from his sister, Stanley looked at his father.

"You killed George. I...saw you shoot him."

"You didn't see any such thing," Carl sneered. "If you had, you'd have told the police, when it happened. When they first questioned you. But you didn't, did you? You didn't, because you never saw anything."

Carl waived his hand at Joan and Stanley, dismissively.

"I don't know what damned game you two are playing, but it won't work. You can't waltz in here and make an accusation like that. No one will believe you."

Okay, I figured it was time for me to get into the discussion. I moved up to where Joan and Stanley were standing, in front of Carl's desk.

"You can deny all you want, Carl," I told him, "but Stanley did see you shoot George. So
let me tell you how it happened. Let me tell you...how you killed George."

I noticed Carl's hands grip the arms of his chair, his muscles again tensing. Good, I thought. We're starting to get through to him.

"I don't think you meant to kill George. I think it was an accident. You two were arguing, your anger got the better of you, and you shot him."

"I don't own a gun," Carl interrupted me.

"It wasn't your gun," I told him. "It was George's."

And then, stretching the truth a bit, I said, "I have a witness ready to swear that George bought the gun from him. Same caliber. And as soon as the police find it, which they will, I'm sure it will turn out to be the murder weapon. Probably have your prints all over it. That is, unless you were smart enough to wipe them off. Did you think to do that, Carl?"

My embellished speech did what it was supposed to do – it shook Carl up. And this time, he couldn't hide it, although he tried mightily.

"I don't know anything about George buying a gun! But even if he did -- so what? What's that got to do with me?"

I ignored his question and continued my description of how

the killing happened.

"When you and George were arguing, you were in his office. For some reason, he took the gun out from his desk. Who knows why? But you're so much bigger and stronger than George, and you wrestled the gun away from him."

"You're blowing smoke!" Carl shouted. "You don't know anything. You don't know what you're talking about!"

"And by that time," I kept going, "you were so angry with George, that you couldn't help yourself. You used his gun, and you shot him. You shot him and you killed him."

"Nothing but lies!" Carl shouted, but his growing agitation was obvious.

"But then," I continued, "you were faced with the problem of what to do? You'd killed George. You hadn't meant to, of course. But there he was. Dead. Laying in his chair."

"I don't have to listen to this crap," Carl said, reaching for the phone on his desk.

I grabbed his wrist and squeezed hard, right on both sides of the wrist bone.

Carl winced, trying not to let the pain show, but I knew I was hurting him.

"No phones," I said. Not until we're through."

Carl glared at me and tried to move his arm. I squeezed harder on his wrist, and pulled his arm away from the phone.

"No phones," I repeated.

When Carl didn't go for the phone again, I continued.

"So, as I was saying, there you were, the gun in your hand, George dead in his chair. What to do? You probably thought about calling the police and explaining the circumstances. After all, things like this can happen. Can be explained. Something could be worked out. Certainly, not a murder charge.

"But then, Carl, that fertile brain of yours saw an opportunity. A one-time opportunity that you just couldn't let go by. A way to fix the money problems Clemson Automotive was having."

"What money problems?" Carl cut in. "We don't have money problems. I built this company, and it's a great company."

I nodded toward Stanley.

"I'm sure when the time comes, with the police, Stanley will verify what I'm saying. And I've also got other sources giving me information. You can deny all you want, but up until a few weeks ago, Clemson Automotive was having cash flow problems. Serious ones. You were slow in paying your suppliers who were thinking about holding back on shipments to you. And you had approached Acme, to ask if they would like to acquire Clemson Automotive."

"You sonofabitch!" Carl spat out.

"That may be," I said pleasantly, knowing that I was finally getting to him, "but what I am, is beside the point.

"Let's just stay on the point, which is, that you saw, in this terrible event, George's death, an opportunity, and you had to take advantage of it. You had to."

I paused for emphasis and then continued.

"Want to tell your children what that opportunity was, Carl? What opportunity George's death offered?"

I waited, but Carl said nothing. I continued.

"You knew that the company carried key man life insurance on you, and on George and Stanley, too. Ten million dollars' worth on each. You knew that, didn't you, Carl?"

Again, I paused, hoping to goad him. But he only glared at me so I went on.

"You had a problem, though. Sure, the insurance would pay off for George's death. But what about you? Here was the opportunity to get the money you needed to save your beloved company. But if things stayed this way, you'd be arrested for murder. Probably go to prison for the rest of your life. And that wouldn't be any good. If you were in prison, how could you use that money to save your company?"

I shook my head from side to side.

"Quite a dilemma, huh Carl?"

I could see Clemson starting to shrivel in his seat. Not much. Just around the fringes. But I sensed that I was edging toward the truth. Toward what really happened.

I picked up my narrative again.

"Well, there was a way out, wasn't there, Carl? You reasoned that if you could make the killing look like part of a robbery, then everything would be fine.

"Of course, George would still be dead, but you would have the ten million you needed, you wouldn't be stuck in prison, and you could revive your company with the money.

"So, you took George's wallet. And you took the gun. Then you called 911 and waited for the police to show up. By the time they did, you had your story all set.

"It was perfect, Carl. Perfect. Only, you didn't know that Stanley saw you kill George. He saw you do it. And while he wouldn't...couldn't...come forward – then -- and tell what he saw, he is ready to do so, now. He's already told Joan and me. I've already told the police and I expect Charlie Black to show up anytime now, and arrest you."

I stopped talking. I'd spun a good story. Maybe even a great story. But what the hell, a lot still depended on how Clemson was going to react.

Yes, we had Stanley's testimony. But let's face it, he wasn't the picture of stability. Despite what he'd say he saw, what he'd swear to, I could picture a hard edged defense attorney getting Stanley to cry on the witness stand, cutting way back on his believability.

"Look at the witness, Ladies and Gentleman," the attorney would say. "Look at the emotional state he is in. I ask you, how much of what he has testified to...is real? Or – only real -- in his mind?"

After I stopped talking, it was quiet. No one spoke. No one moved.

Then Joan, the one child of Carl's who most resembled him in toughness and smarts, confronted her father,

"How could you do it!" she demanded. "How could you kill your own son? And then treat the whole thing like a...a damned business decision! Your own son!" she shouted at him.

I decided it was time to kick Carl in the balls, pun absolutely intended.

"Maybe he found the whole thing easier to do," I said, "because George wasn't his son."

Joan and Stanley were stunned.

And I could see Carl starting to come apart now, as he guessed, feared, what I meant.

"I don't understand..." Joan said.

"I'm sorry," I said to her and to Stanley. "I'm sorry you have to learn about it this way. But the fact is, while your mother is

George's birth mother, your father is not George's birth father."

I went on to tell them what Bill Schlesinger had told me, about the encounter Emily Clemson had with the pharmacist, Richard Bellows, with George being the result,

And about Carl's low sperm count, and his decision to claim paternity.

It was time for the final pressure point.

"Come in, Charlie," I called toward the hall.

Charlie Black came into the office.

"Did you get it all?" I asked.

Charlie held up a still-running tape recorder.

"Every beautiful word."

He looked at Carl.

"Mr. Clemson, I want you to come with me to the station, for questioning related to the death of your son, George Clemson."

Charlie started reading Clemson his Miranda rights.

"You have the right..." he began...

"Wait! Clemson cut him off."

Charlie stopped. Clemson nodded at me, and then he spoke to Joan and Stanley.

"He had some of it right," he told them, "but nowhere near everything."

"You have the right..." Charlie began again, aware that a defense attorney could get everything Clemson said from now on, tossed out, if Clemson wasn't properly Mirandized.

Clemson interrupted him again.

"All right. For the record, I, Carl Clemson, acknowledge that you have advised me of my rights. But...and I want to talk. I want to talk."

"You waive your right to remain silent?" Charlie persisted. "And you waive your right to an attorney being present?"

"Yes, I waive those rights. And any other rights I may have."

Charlie was satisfied.

"Okay, go ahead," he told Clemson.

Carl said, "Here is how it really happened. I was in my office, I heard a loud bang, I went out to the hall, and I saw George's light on, in his office.

"I went into his office and George was in his chair. Behind his desk. He'd shot himself.

"I ran over to the desk. I wasn't sure if he was alive or dead, and I wanted to see if there was anything I could do. You have to believe me, I wanted to help George.

"But he was dead. His...part of his head was...blown away." He paused and looked at Joan and Stanley. "He was beyond help, then. He was dead. You understand? He was dead."

Clemson looked at me.

"Yes, you're right about what I did, then. About setting it up to look like a robbery. I had to."

"But I saw you shoot George!" Stanley cried. "I saw you shoot him. Twice!"

"I had to," Carl repeated. "I had to."

Suddenly, Joan reached across the desk and slapped her father, hard, driving him back into his chair.

"So you put two more bullets into George after he was dead? Just to meet your business plan? How could you! How could you!"

Charlie walked around Clemson's desk with a set of open handcuffs.

"Stand up," he ordered,

Clemson stood, and Charlie turned him around and put on the cuffs.

"Okay," he shouted toward the hall outside the office, and two LAPD officers came in and took positions on either side of Clemson.

"Mr. Clemson," Charlie said, "I am taking you back to the station, for questioning, in connection with the death of George Clemson."

Charlie read Clemson the full Miranda rights statement, then asked, " Do you understand?"

Clemson nodded, and then said, clearly and with emphasis, "No more questions until I have my lawyer present. I'm not answering any questions until then."

Carl's demand – and yes, that's what it was – got my attention, and I took a close look at him. What I saw was a calm man. Not someone who had just admitted shooting his son, and who had then been slapped and yelled at, by his daughter.

I reviewed in my mind the last few minutes, and I saw what I suspected Clemson had realized, there at the end. That about the only thing against him was – that he had admitted shooting George two more times, after George – he claimed – had committed suicide. And who could say, it didn't go down that way? Especially since the second and third shots were what Stanley had seen.

I had hoped that having Joan and Stanley confront Carl would result in an admission by Carl that he had killed George. But that didn't happen. Carl even rejected my theory about the argument and his having shot George, initially in anger, and then two more times in an attempted cover-up. Instead, he had offered his version of George's death, starting with the suicide.

Give him that much credit, I thought to myself. He is one tough son of a bitch. Down one minute. But back up and fighting, the next.

Charlie called me at home that evening.

"He's out. We maybe could have kept him the full 24, but his lawyer pushed hard. And about all D.A Groverman would go for at this point, is further investigation to determine if there is a probable cause for a charge of tampering with the evidence at the scene."

"So he's out," I repeated. "What about flight risk?"

"Groverman said he wasn't worried. Substantial businessman, ties to the community, the usual bullshit."

"You think the tampering charge will stick?"

"Well, we got him on tape, with his version of George's death – that George committed suicide, and then Carl shot George two more times. If that isn't tampering with the scene, then I don't know what is.

"But on the other hand, his lawyer's already pushing the angle that Carl wasn't properly Mirandized, He's also saying he wants to question Stanley. He smells the weakness there. And he's claiming that Carl was traumatized by seeing his son dead, and he should not be held accountable for his subsequent actions."

"This is going to be a long haul," I said. "And he might get out of it. Or mostly out of it. Maybe something suspended, with community service thrown in."

"Sounds about right," Charlie agreed.

"Do Joan, Stanley and Emily know all this?"

"I just saw them.

"How'd they take it?"

"They asked me a lot of questions. And then they were pissed – when they realized how this could end up. With Carl maybe beating any rap."

Chapter Thirty-Six

After Charlie and I had finished talking, I called Joan Clemson at home, but only reached her voice mail. I left a message.

A few days went by, I tried Joan at home, at her office, and at her parent's home in Silver Ridge. Never got through, left messages, no call-back.

So I concentrated on my other cases – until a week later, when the Carl Clemson case came right back up to the top of my attention list.

Carl Clemson, according to the morning TV newscast I was watching while eating breakfast, had been found dead – in his bed, at home. Cause of death not yet known.

Later that day, Charlie filled me in.

"The coroner hasn't finished his autopsy report yet, but the preliminary is, that Carl died from an overdose of that pain killer you told me about – Avinza."

"Does the coroner think it was accidental or suicide?"

"I think it will probably end up being ruled, accidental. There was a pill bottle on the night table next to his bed, and not all the pills in the bottle were consumed. And usually, an empty pill bottle is a strong sign of a suicide. Plus, for whatever it's worth, I saw Carl close up enough times, and I don't think he was the suicide type. What do you think?"

"I agree."

I switched subjects.

"You said, 'his bedroom,' not theirs?"

"Right. They had separate bedrooms."

"Who found him?"

"His wife."

Chapter Thirty-Seven

Carl's funeral was a few days later. Family only, with a reception to follow, at the Clemson home. I decided to go. I wanted to express my condolences in person.

In contrast to the last funeral reception – the one for George – this one was smaller and more subdued. When I came in, I saw Emily Clemson, sitting with Joan, on the same couch as at the last reception. This time, though, Emily looked different.

It took me a minute to figure out the difference. And then, I saw it.

Emily was dry-eyed. No tears. No mourning. No indication that she might be on an anti-depressant.

Instead, she looked – strong. No longer seemingly dominated by the force that had been Carl.

I walked over to the couch.

"I'm sorry for your loss," I said to Emily and Joan, the usual police department comment still in my system.

Emily nodded. "Thank you."

A small, cool smile, and then she shifted topics.

"I understand you knew Carl was taking Avinza?

"Yes."

Emily shook her head

"Too bad he didn't pay attention to the warnings in the prescription literature."

"What warnings?" I asked.

"The warnings about the need to take only the smallest possible dosage," Emily said. "And the dangers of overdosing."

Emily sighed.

"But that was typical of Carl, wasn't it? Not to pay attention to instructions from others. Not to care what others said or recommended. But to do things only the way he wanted to do them."

Emily shook her head again.

"Unfortunately, that habit caught up with him, this time, didn't it?"

I stared at Emily.

No flicker of anything on an impassive face.

I looked at Joan.

Her face was a reflection of her mother's.

They both stared at me, silently.

There didn't seem to be anything more to say – so I left.

On the way back to my office, I replayed what I had just seen and heard.

Do you remember that old English saying:

"Hell has no fury like a woman scorned."

Well, Emily Clemson sure was a woman scorned by Carl – in more ways than one.

Which led me to wonder, was that – fury – that I had seen her display back there?

If so, then…about Carl's death…maybe…

Whoa! I cautioned myself. You really don't want to go there…

Additional books by Saul Warshaw

From pre-World War Two Poland, to the polish partisan bands that fought the occupying German army during the War, from the fabled Lower East side of New York City in the late 1940's, to present day Los Angeles and New York. That's the time and geographic spread that Will Jones, private investigator and retired LAPD homicide detective, must grapple with, on behalf of his clients, a brother and sister who have read in their grandmother's just discovered diary -- her confession that she killed her husband. It's a confession they don't want to believe about their beloved, recently deceased Bubby (Jewish Grandmother). But the fact is - their grandfather's murder in New York in 1948 has never been solved. The brother and sister hire Will to find the real killer, hoping that when he does so, this will disprove, even if it does not explain, their grandmother's confession. But, suppose this is a killing that some people never want to be solved, despite Will's efforts to do so?

Businessmen are being murdered in different parts of Los Angeles in seemingly unrelated homicides. Will Jonas, formerly an LAPD homicide detective and now a private investigator, is hired by the family of one of the victims, because they are dissatisfied with the lack of progress of the LAPD investigation. Working with his former LAPD partner, who is still on the Job, Will finds a common thread tying together the killings, discovers the surprisingly unusual motive for the homicides and nails the killer. A KILLING IN BUSINESS is the second Will Jonas mystery thriller, following last year's KILLING MEMORIES.

Excerpt from A Killing in Business

The Year: 1999

Prolog

It was one of those midwinter heat waves that always hit Los Angeles, and even now, close to 1:00 a.m., with the Santa Ana winds still gusting out of the north, the temperature in the San Fernando Valley was in the mid-seventies.

Lionel Anderson turned off Ventura Boulevard in Woodland Hills and drove south, toward his house, three blocks south of the Boulevard.

The top was down on his Mercedes 530 SL and he was smiling. The meeting with the investor had gone well, and it looked like he would pull through his latest money scrape just fine.

Never mind that what he'd told the guy wasn't exactly the way things really were. He could straighten that part out later, especially once the information on the twins started paying off. What was important right now, was to keep the money flowing.

Lionel guided the Benz into his driveway, parked behind his wife, Charisse's Plymouth Voyager, and then grimaced as he looked at his house. Typical of this part of Woodland Hills, eighteen hundred square feet of cookie cutter tract housing.

Well, he thought, just a little more time, a few more of the right moves, and he and his family would be living in one of those million-dollar jobs in Calabasas. Maybe even up in the two or three million dollar class.

His housing dream was interrupted as the silencer-equipped gun pressed up against the side of his head. Lionel tried to turn, but the pressure from the gun kept him from doing so.

"Hey, what do you want?" he managed to ask, before the bullet ripped into his skull, shredding most of his brain.

Chapter One

"It's been eight months since our son was murdered, and the police haven't done anything," Melinda Anderson complained to me. "Nothing at all."

Added her husband, James, "Because he was black, it's like Lionel's being killed don't count. Was a white man shot down like that, in front of his house, his wife and baby sleeping inside, the police would be paying attention."

The Andersons glared at me, their looks challenging me to disagree.

Mrs. Anderson looked every bit the grade school teacher she'd told me she was. A bit on the plump side, she was wearing a dark brown dress and sensible brown shoes, the kind you need when you're on your feet most of the day.

Mr, Anderson, a US Post Office delivery man, was wearing his uniform. He was tall, around six feet, lean and fit, looking like all that walking was good for him.

I took the Andersons up on their challenge.

"I don't buy what you're claiming. Sure, back in the 40's and 50's, you'd be right. And even later, too. But since Rodney King, it's not that way. And it wasn't my way, when I was on the Job."

I'm Will Jonas, retired after 30 years with the Los Angeles Police Department, and into my fourth year as a private investigator.

"What about all those drive-by shootings in South Central?" Mrs. Anderson said. "How many of those get solved?"

I couldn't blame the Andersons for their views. They'd lost a son to an unknown killer and here it was, eight months later, with no progress on the case.

"You're right about South Central," I conceded. "The Department tries, but there are too many shootings down there for anyone to handle. Your son, though, he was killed in Woodland Hills, in a good neighborhood. If the police haven't turned up anything, I'm sure it's not because they haven't been trying."

James Anderson put a hand on his wife's shoulder.

"Mr. Jonas, we get carried away about Lionel…and what happened to him. We know it's not as bad as it used to be. But you have to understand, Lionel's our son, our only child. And when we read that story about you in the paper, well, we're hoping you can help us."

The story in the paper? A couple of Sundays ago, the L.A. Times did one of those "Where are they now?" articles, about people who'd been in the news at one time or another. When I was with LAPD, especially the last 10 years on Homicide, I was the lead detective on some high profile cases. Got a lot of publicity at the time.

When the Times reporter called, I agreed to the interview, figuring it might be good for business. And here's the result of the article, sitting in front of me – the Andersons, grieving for their son Lionel, and angry that the Department hadn't been able to find his killer.

If it's the money you're concerned about," Mr. Anderson said, "we can pay. We make good salaries, and we got savings."

"No, it's not the money," I said. "I'm just not sure I can do anything for you."

"Why is that?" Mrs. Anderson asked.

"Because, hard as it may be for you to accept, it is possible that your son's killing may not be solvable. The fact is, if a homicide doesn't get solved in the first few days, or if, at the least, there aren't some good leads in that time period, then it's tough to get any results. It's been eight months. Everything about your son's case is cold. I'm sure the police have done everything they could, and I don't see what I can do, so long after the fact."

Mrs. Anderson leaned forward, almost across my desk, in close to me, working hard not to cry.

"Or grandson is three years old now," she said. "And he's asking questions of our daughter-in-law, and of us. 'Where's my Daddy? What happened to my Daddy?' How is his mother – and how are we – supposed to answer those questions, Mr. Jonas? Our daughter-in-law needs answers. We need answers. Please help us."

Could I resist a plea like that from a grieving grandmother?